A FLI

Although not originally intent on becoming a children's author, Geoffrey Trease, born in 1909, has always loved writing and history, and was able to combine the two in his first children's novel, *Bows Against the Barons*, published in 1934. He is now the celebrated author of some eighty children's books and a number of adult works, including novels and a history of London. His works have appeared in twenty-six countries and twenty languages and many were dramatised as radio serials in the BBC's *Children's Hour*.

Geoffrey Trease has travelled widely in Europe, lived in Russia, and served in India in the Second World War. He now lives in Bath, next door to his daughter, Jocelyn. He also has four granddaughters, twin great-granddaughters and a great-grandson – but, as he says, 'no other pets'!

Other books by Geoffrey Trease

The Aprino Assignment
Bows Against the Barons
Calabrian Quest
Cue For Treason
Shadow Under the Sea
Tomorrow is a Stranger
The White Nights of St Petersburg
The Popinjay Mystery
Aunt Augusta's Elephant

A FLIGHT OF OF ANGELS

Geoffrey Trease

Illustrated by Eric Stemp

PIPER
PAN MACMILLAN
CHILDREN'S BOOKS

First published 1988 by Macmillan Children's Books

This Piper edition published 1993 by Pan Macmillan Children's Books
a division of Pan Macmillan Publishers Limited
Cavaye Place London SW10 9PG
and Basingstoke

Associated companies throughout the world

ISBN 0 330 32581 7

1 3 5 7 9 8 6 4 2

A CIP catalogue record for this book is available from
the British Library

Typeset by Universe Typesetters
Printed in England by Clays Ltd, St Ives plc

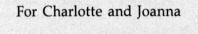

For Charlotte and Joanna

Author's Note

This story is inspired by the real
sandstone caves that underlie the inner
city of Nottingham. Mortimer's Hole at
the castle can be visited. And the town
was famous for its alabaster carvers in the
Middle Ages.

Chapter One

"Not much of a secret passage, if you ask *me*!"

"No one *is* asking you, Rodney."

Mrs Ledbury's usually pleasant voice had a slight edge. She liked the class to express their opinions freely, but it had been a long morning. And Rodney Walsh could be an awkward little devil.

The whole castle, according to him, was not much of a castle. Even Sheila, who liked history, was always disappointed in it. No ruined turrets, no battlements, just a huge mansion really. "Charles the Second's reign, 1679," Mrs Ledbury had told them, and the class had dutifully scribbled the date on their clipboards.

Nowadays it was the city museum. Sheila would have preferred the real castle that had stood there before, the one Richard Lionheart had once besieged. Nothing of that remained but the massive gatehouse with its twin round towers. And the secret passage.

Mrs Ledbury had kept that to the end, after they had toured the endless galleries with their oil paintings and showcases.

The green uniformed guide had been waiting for them outside in the crisp March breeze. They straggled along, pausing only to peer over a low parapet at the city far below. At least the site of the vanished fortress was still impressive, a huge brown crag, falling at this point in an almost sheer precipice.

1

"A hundred and thirty feet," said Mrs Ledbury, who had clearly mugged up all the answers. But she would not discuss the suicides who, as every one knew, chucked themselves off once in a while.

"Only once each," muttered someone. Mrs Ledbury could not help smiling herself, but she quelled the giggles and reminded them that the guide was waiting.

Rodney's comment, "Not much of a secret passage", seemed a fair one. There was a board with times and admission charges, there were railings, and a flight of steps leading down to a door set in the rock. "Looks more like the way to the Gents," said Rodney. "You girls better hang back a bit!"

"Pipe down," said Mrs Ledbury, "or you won't hear what the guide's going to tell us."

There was electric light inside. "Very romantic," said Rodney. "Genuine medieval!"

Sheila was rather relieved. She had been nerving herself for something more scary. Darkness and bats – a bat tangling in her mop of hair – ugh! But there were no bats, or snakes, or skeletons.

Only their own shadows danced grotesquely on the arched rock overhead, thrown up by lights set at ground level along the sides of the passage. It was all dry and clean, without any musty smell.

"It's the sandstone," the teacher explained. "All this part of Nottingham lies on sandstone. It's very porous, the rainwater soaks through, so you get natural caves – and the rock is very easy to cut if you need to."

There were steps cut in the steeper places. The guide said that the passage ran right down to the base of the precipice. A hundred yards long, it was.

He gathered the party round him. "In olden times this was a private back way out of the castle." He launched himself into the story of how it came to be called Mortimer's Hole.

In 1330 the most powerful baron in England was Roger Mortimer. Not just because he was a great lord, but because he had so much influence over Queen Isabella.

"Why— " someone started to ask.

"He was what *you'd* call her boyfriend," said Mrs Ledbury quickly. "You don't have to beat about the bush with these children," she assured the guide. "They know the facts of life."

"Didn't the King have anything to say about it?" asked Debby Harker.

The guide stared, and Debby stared back at him cheerfully, brown eyes dancing, white teeth flashing with fun. She knew she was the smallest girl in the class, but if he thought she was a little kid he had another think coming. She seldom asked questions in history lessons – her family came from Jamaica and she didn't see that English history was anything much to do with her. But at the first whiff of scandal she was alert.

"If she was the Queen," Debby argued, "she must have had a husband who was King, right? And he couldn't have been much of a King if he let her run around with—"

"Just a moment, love. Her husband was dead. Edward the Second, that was — "

"He'd been bumped off, hadn't he?" said Rodney.

"Yes ... Well—"

"How did they do him in?" Rodney loved a good murder.

"We must stick to the point," said Mrs Ledbury hurriedly, "or we'll be here all day."

No one wanted that. Rodney shut up. The man went on, "His son was rightly King, now, Edward the Third, but he wasn't eighteen yet, so his mother was running the country for him."

"And this Mortimer was running *her*?" said Debby.

The guide pretended not to hear. "The situation couldn't go on much longer," he continued, "because the lad was getting near his eighteenth birthday—"

"Ah!" breathed Debby with heavy significance.

"Which wasn't going to suit his mother — or Mortimer."

The class were now quite tense. This might be history but it was life all right. "What was Isabella like?" Sheila asked.

"Oh, a good looker. They called her 'the rose among the fairest' when she first came over from France to get married. But she soon showed she'd got thorns as well. Then her enemies called her 'the she-wolf of France'. Her father was King of France. Anyhow, she didn't fancy handing over to her son and taking a back seat. Nor did Mortimer."

"It'd be curtains for *him*," said Rodney. "Obviously."

"Everybody was planning for that special birthday — but in different ways," said the guide with sinister emphasis. "Mortimer wasn't going to let go that easy. He'd filled the castle with his own supporters and he'd got everything under control — he thought. He was planning a *coup* — like they're always having in foreign countries nowadays. Every night, when the castle gates

4

were locked, the keys were taken to Isabella's bedchamber."

"Why not Mortimer's?" asked Debby, all innocent looking.

"Be your age," Rodney begged her.

"But Edward had plenty of friends," the guide was explaining hurriedly, "and they tipped him off about what Mortimer was cooking up. One of them – William de Montacute – took him aside and said, 'Better to eat the dog than let the dog eat us!' There was no time to lose, with the birthday only a month away, so they picked that very night and made a project."

The last word brought groans from the entire class. The guide looked mystified. "Don't mind them," said Mrs Ledbury, "it's the mention of 'projects'. I set them all a project to work on in the Easter holidays."

There were more groans, though much of the lamentation was put on. Sheila herself was quite looking forward to the project and wondering what topic her group would be given. It had to be local history. It might be fun to write about Mortimer's Hole.

The guide went on with his story. "All the King's friends – like Montacute – had to be out of the castle by locking-up time. Edward had to stay in. He was almost a prisoner – treated respectfully, of course, but Mortimer didn't want him getting into mischief. Still, Montacute managed to get a private word with him, and they made this proj— – I mean, this plan."

He paused, and there was a chorus of impatient questions.

"One at a time, now! You first, Curlytop."

Sheila didn't much like this description, but she knew

5

he could only mean her. "Did they know about this passage?"

"A local man told them, William d'Eland. He was in charge of the castle just then, so Montacute put it to him very straight, 'You've got to help us,' he said. 'Leave a gate unlocked or something, so we can get back in during the night. It's your bounden duty,' he said, 'Edward's your King, your liege lord. If you won't help him now you'll swing for it when he comes to power. Only next month!'"

"Straight talk," agreed Rodney with approval. "I bet this bloke said yes."

"Yes – and he had an even better idea. There was this secret way in. If they'd creep through the deer park after midnight he'd meet them at the foot of the precipice and bring them in through the secret door. He'd lead them up through this passage where we're standing, and they'd come out at the top in the castle courtyard, as it was then."

"And this truly happened, sir?"

That was the voice of Kanshi Ram. Kanshi had a passion for accuracy. He was a wizard at maths, but normally, like Debby, he was not much interested in English history. His people, too, had come from somewhere else. India.

"Would I tell you if it didn't?" demanded the guide. "October the nineteenth, it was. 1330." Pencils and clipboards were active. "Edward's birthday was November the thirteenth."

"Did it go off OK?" asked Debby.

"Worked like a charm, love. They crept up here – all in armour, with their swords – and the lad was waiting for them at the top. But Mortimer was still awake, plotting with his henchmen in the room next to the Queen's bedchamber."

The class listened, breathless. The guide warmed to the tale he must have told so often. Edward and his friends tiptoed through the torch-lit passages. Then suddenly the alarm was raised. Someone yelled "Traitors!" and there was a servant barring their way with a dagger. Someone settled him. Then they burst in on Mortimer.

"And settled *him*?" asked Rodney hopefully.

"Not then and there."

"I'll bet he was for the chop, though."

"You might say the outlook was poor," agreed the guide. "He was taken up to London and tried and condemned. He wasn't actually 'for the chop', as you say – they hanged him at Tyburn as a common criminal."

"Did the young King ever speak to his mum again?" Sheila enquired.

"Must have done. After all, she was the Queen Mother. So, as long as she didn't meddle any more, she had to be treated properly."

Some of the class murmured their disappointment. Isabella did not fit their idea of a good mum.

"But if her father was King of France," Kanshi reminded them, "the new King of England would have to go carefully."

The guide led them on. It was a good hundred yards to the end of the passage at the foot of the cliff. As they made the steep climb back, Sheila tackled Mrs Ledbury.

"I was wondering – if the others agreed – could we do

this passage as our project?"

"Hm ... " Mrs Ledbury considered as they picked their way carefully up some uneven rocky steps. "You're supposed to do research – look things up, put two and two together. I think the guide has told us pretty well all that's known. If you only retell the story in your own words it wouldn't make much of a project."

"I s'pose not," said Sheila regretfully.

Mrs Ledbury liked a project to be a challenge. Lots of books to look up, indexes, visits to the public library ... Probably this incident of Mortimer's Hole did not offer enough scope for that.

But the subterranean journey through the Castle Rock lingered in Sheila's imagination. She was still full of it at tea-time when her father came in.

"This man said that the whole city centre is built on sandstone, not just the castle," she said. "He reckoned there's caves under lots of shops and pubs and offices. Do you think that's true, Dad?"

"I know it is," said Mr Drake, taking another slice of bread. "Don't I work in caves myself, every day of my life?"

Chapter Two

Sheila stared. "You mean at Peblow's? The cellars?"

"Cellars – or caves. Who's to say which?" said her father comfortably, as he spread the butter liberally. "They may have started as caves. Then, very likely, people cut away the rock to make 'em larger. Mr Peblow reckons there was once an inn there. Our cellars may be as old as this Mortimer's Hole."

"You never told me!"

"You never showed that much interest in your dad's place of work," said Mrs Drake. It was true. Sheila had always taken her father's job for granted, like her sister's office or her brother's apprenticeship at the printer's.

Peblow's was an old-fashioned little place in a twisty byway on Gillyflower Hill, near the castle gates. Mr Peblow was a wine and spirit merchant. "On his own," Mr Drake always insisted, "and that's rare nowadays with all these chains and the supermarkets."

Mr Drake was his cellarman. It meant keeping a close check on the stock. Some of it was very valuable, for the rarer wines were highly priced. "Like drinking liquid gold," Mum used to say.

The job meant a lot of running up and down the steep cellar steps, and heaving heavy cases about. Dad thought nothing of that. He wasn't a big man, but his tattooed arms had the strength of a gorilla's. He had been a merchant seaman once. Then he'd met Mum, and had quickly decided to find a steady job ashore.

Peblow's was certainly that. Some might have called it dull, but it suited Dad. "Had my bellyful of the romance of the sea," he'd say with a chuckle. "Your mum beat that hollow."

"Go on with you," Mum would say, but she always looked pleased.

Now Dad leant across the table and said, "Tell you what, Sheila, if you're so keen on these old places, why not come down and see for yourself?"

"Could I, Dad?"

"Do you think you ought, Sam?" Mum broke in doubtfully. "Would Mr Peblow like children going round his precious cellars?"

"Sheila's not 'children', Mother. She's my daughter."

"All the same, do you think—"

"I think", said Dad with dignity, "that if he trusts me with those cellar keys he trusts me to decide who's OK to take down there."

"I shouldn't start smashing bottles," Sheila promised. "It's only the caves I want to see."

"I could take you Sunday morning," he suggested.

"You don't go in on Sundays," said Mum.

"This Sunday I must. I've a bit of rearrangement to do, shifting stock around. Need peace and quiet for that." He turned back to Sheila. "You got your paper round. When you done that, come on down. You can have a peep round without bothering anybody."

"Thanks, Dad. I'd like that."

She always did like doing things with Dad. They had a sort of special relationship, partly because Mum

11

worked different shifts at the hospital, and some weeks Sheila had to get a meal ready for her father. They often had good talks together.

Her brother Kevin wasn't there much. If at home, he was forever out in the back yard, endlessly tinkering with his motorbike. At other times he was out with the lads. And her big sister, Glenda, shared a flat with two other girls. Sheila still missed her, but enjoyed having a bedroom to herself.

So a date was fixed with her father for Sunday morning. A new idea was forming in her mind. Next Monday, Mrs Ledbury would be approving the projects each group was to work on.

Mortimer's Hole was too easy. But suppose Sheila got her group to suggest a project about all the caves and cellars lying beneath the modern city? Who'd used them, when, and what for? Bags of scope there for the kind of research Mrs Ledbury was so hot on. She felt sure she could sell the idea to Mrs Ledbury. But could she sell it to her group?

She was teamed up with Debby, Rodney and Kanshi Ram. Mrs Ledbury liked a good balance of the sexes and the races.

Debby wouldn't be difficult. A cheerful, good-humoured girl, she'd go along with what the others wanted. Kanshi might take more persuading. He could be prickly and argue a lot, especially if a girl tried to take the lead.

Rodney would be an even tougher nut to crack. If she could win him over, she'd have less difficulty with Kanshi. He admired Rodney. If Rodney liked the project, Kanshi would probably fall into line.

So she must work on Rodney – and before Monday's lesson. No good boring Rodney with a lot of chat about history. He'd need something more solid to arouse his interest.

What could be more solid than the rock-hewn walls of Peblow's wine cellars?

It was lucky that Rodney did a Sunday paper round for the same shop. They often went into the park afterwards and met schoolfriends before going home to dinner.

When Sunday came it all worked out. Dead easy.

Sheila said casually, "I'm meeting my dad at Peblow's. He's going to show me the cellars. They're sort of caves really, adapted."

"I'll walk you down through the town then," he answered, as she'd hoped.

They sauntered through the deserted shopping streets, crossed the great square, and turned up the narrow lane that ran up to the castle. Peblow's stood in a shabby row of run-down old properties. There was a lawyer's office on one side and a jeweller's on the other, then a second-hand bookshop and a place selling old-fashioned junk that collectors went crazy over.

They found Mr Drake in the paved yard, overshadowed by tall grimy buildings like cliffs all around. Today the yard was piled high with crumpled cartons and broken cases, splintered shelving and littered straw.

"You *have* been having a clear out," said Sheila.

"Not before time. But I'm nearly done. If you and Rodney like to come down – "

They followed him across the yard, down a flight of

steps, and through an open doorway at the bottom. Inside, the steps continued, not flagged but cut in the tawny rock like those in Mortimer's Hole. Mr Drake reached for a switch. On their left a rugged archway suddenly lit up, disclosing a circular vault with a rough-hewn column of sandstone rising in the centre.

"We call this the Pillar Cave," he said. "We reckon it was natural, but they enlarged it ages ago to make a cellar. They left this pillar standing so as the roof wouldn't fall in on them."

"It's like a church almost," said Rodney.

"Well, Miss Jenny – Mr Peblow's daughter, that is – *she's* the one with the ideas – she wants to have it all tidied up and furnished. Then they can bring down regular customers and hold wine-tasting parties and all that. Got to move with the times, she says. But Mr Peblow takes some budgin'. Sort of set in his ways, he is."

Sheila pictured the Pillar Cave as Miss Jenny wanted it. Subdued lights instead of that naked bulb. Rugs underfoot, hangings to soften the rock walls. Ruby red wine, or golden, twinkling through cut glass. Miss Jenny would know how to do things. Daughters could often teach their fathers.

Wistfully she followed the others down a second flight of steps into a complex of three connecting cellars. Here were thousands of bottles lying on their sides, claret and burgundy, hock and champagne, port and sherry and Madeira.

Dad pointed out some of the old-time bins that still survived. "Bins" were really brick-lined benches or thralls, running along the cellar-sides, with rows of

14

horizontal bottles supported by those beneath them. For many years now, though, wine merchants had been changing over to racks of wood or metal.

"Do you have to carry everything up all those steps?" asked Rodney sympathetically.

"Not on your life, lad! Maybe they did in bygone days, but we've a lift now – just a little goods lift to take a few cases of wine." Mr Drake showed them the lift shaft. They stuck their heads in and peered up at a narrow chink of daylight far above.

"Must have been quite a job," said Rodney, "cutting down through all that rock!"

But Mr Drake believed they had merely adapted an ancient well shaft that had been there already. Mr Peblow said that in the Middle Ages most houses in this part of the town had had their own wells.

They came to the cellar where Mr Drake had been working. He pointed to the priceless stock of vintage port ranged in its new steel racks. He showed them how each bottle carried a white smudge on one side, which must always be kept uppermost, so that the sediment should not be stirred up. He'd moved all this stock, bottle by bottle, as tenderly as if each one was a new-born baby. Now, in the dark corner against the far wall, he had only to finish dismantling the old wooden racks where they had lain undisturbed, some of them since long before he had joined the firm.

Sheila and Rodney helped him to remove the last of the racks that had now served their purpose. Suddenly the boy exclaimed, "Got a torch, Mr Drake? Or a box of matches?"

"What's up? Dropped something?" Mr Drake

lumbered across good-humouredly, and flashed the torch he always kept handy in case of a power failure.

"Look at the wall here! 'Tisn't rock. It's proper stonework. There's a sort of archway."

Mr Drake did not share Rodney's excitement. But he agreed. "That's right. So there is."

Instead of the rough sandstone there were smooth blocks of a different, greyish stone, well-shaped blocks neatly mortared together. Sheila's eyes followed the sweep of Rodney's hand as it traced the curve of an archway. It was just an outline, a frame for the masonry that filled it in completely from side to side.

"Must have been a doorway here," said Rodney. "Must be another cave behind."

"Most likely there was, at one time," said Mr Drake placidly. "But not in my day – nor Mr Peblow's, I'll be bound."

"Why would it be blocked up?" The excitement in Rodney's voice suggested that his imagination was running away with him.

"Safety, maybe. They might have had a rock fall and be scared of having another. Or they just didn't need the extra cellarage. So they walled it off, and stored stuff in front of it, and gradually every one forgot it had ever been there."

"Dad!" Sheila was crouching, fingering a stone block at ground level. "Would you shine your light here, please?"

He did so.

"There's something carved on the stone!" cried Rodney.

"A big letter V," said Sheila. "I wonder what that was for."

Chapter Three

"V for Victory?" said Rodney.

Sheila's father thought not. "That saying didn't come in till Winston Churchill in the war. These old racks were put in long before – and then nobody could have got at the wall."

"A Roman number five?" Sheila suggested, her fancy beginning to run away with her. "It might go back to the Romans!"

Rodney brought her quickly down to earth. "You can have Roman numbers on anything – like a clock. You don't need an ancient Roman to make 'em."

She had to admit the common sense of that. But the archway, and even the later masonry that now filled it in, looked very old.

It was a neat V, cut by a real craftsman, her father said. Could have been there for centuries. Most likely it *was* just a number.

"The cellar beyond *would* have been the fifth, if you count the Pillar Cave as number one."

"There's just one weakness in that theory," Rodney objected. He read a lot of detective stories.

"And what's that, lad?"

"The V isn't on the archway. It's on this block of stone. Why number the cellar when you've just closed it off and stopped using it?"

"Well, we'll never know, will we?" Mr Drake was

thinking more of his Sunday dinner. "Can't say I'm that bothered."

Rodney was not exactly bothered, but the unanswered question niggled in his mind. He liked mysteries – but he liked to solve them. He would have loved to see that archway opened up again, to reveal what lay beyond.

Not a hope, though, he told himself sadly. Demolishing that masonry would be hard work. He knew that, because his own father was a builder in a small way. Also, by all accounts, Mr Peblow was a pernickety old gentleman. He wouldn't fancy sledgehammers bashing about so near his wine.

"Seen all you want, then?" Mr Drake wanted to get away. "You two go on. I must switch off the lights and lock up."

They climbed the steps into the yard and waited for him in the sunlit lane. The jeweller's window was shuttered, but the bookshop displayed its rows of faded volumes and there was a fascinating medley of odd items in the junkshop beyond. A cat dozed on a doorstep. Otherwise, on this Sunday morning, there was no sign of life on Gillyflower Hill.

Suddenly, though, there was a car. "Mind out!" cried Rodney protectively, grabbing Sheila's arm and pulling her out of the gutter on to the tiny strip of pavement.

It was a very grand car. He felt admiration, as well as anger, at the arrogance with which it surged up the lane, heedless of other people's safety. It swished on round the next bend, and must have braked just out of his view. He heard doors slam. A moment later two men came strolling back.

One, the younger looking, was explaining something in an eager tone. His companion, who wore sun glasses, was merely nodding. The young one pointed up at the tall buildings with their blank dusty windows. Rodney caught the words "Victorian—Regency—Georgian maybe" – the sort of words sightseers used. Only the strangers were not dressed casually as if on holiday. They wore suits and ties, the younger one nothing remarkable, but his companion somehow expensive looking, matching that car.

Their behaviour roused Rodney's curiosity. They were looking particularly at Peblow's, but not at the rather stately upper storeys or the shop frontage with its dignified display of bottles. Their eyes were on the pavement. The man in sun glasses began to walk with a slow, measured pace. It probably was truly a "measured" pace, for the younger man had stopped his flow of chatter, and when the other one halted, sharply, like a sentry, he jotted something down in a notebook.

He had halted exactly where Peblow's ended and Harringay's, the jeweller's, began.

"Wonder who they are," Rodney whispered.

"Men from the Council?" Sheila suggested.

"Working on a Sunday? An' driving a car like that?"

"Well, architects. Planners or something."

"Planners – I'll say they could be planners! Planning a break-in! Crooks. Casing the joint on a quiet Sunday morning when there's nobody about."

"But *we're* about."

"They don't count kids. Barely notice 'em. You saw – they nearly ran over you."

"I think we should tell Dad."

"You're right, we should. Suspicious characters. Never know."

They pretended to be studying the junkshop window, but they kept the strangers under observation. The younger one was talking again, faster, over eager, thought Rodney, over keen. Like a teacher's pet, sucking up to teacher. Rodney knew the type, he recognised the style. He'd seen it at school.

In his mind he was composing a description of both men in case his help should be needed by the police.

This time it was his turn, not Sheila's, to have a romantic fantasy shattered by humdrum reality. The younger man had seen that the yard gates were ajar. He beckoned – but very respectfully – to his companion. At that very moment Sheila's father came out, keys in hand, and met them face to face.

It was a surprise for everybody, but especially for Rodney, when the young man said – covering his confusion with a rather uppish manner – "Ah, Drake! Didn't expect to find *you* here on a Sunday morning!"

"Nor me you, Mr Simon. Just been doing a little extra job for your father. He's not here himself. Were you hoping to see him?"

"No, no, I wouldn't say that." The young man turned to his companion with a chuckle, which sounded to Rodney faintly odd.

"I'll just tell him tomorrow that you called by, then?"

"No need, Drake, no need to mention it at all."

It was fascinating – and rather sickening – the way the man could switch from his teacher's pet tone to the high and mighty manner with which he put Sheila's father in his place.

Mr Drake answered respectfully. "Whatever you say, Mr Simon."

He locked the gates behind him. The men walked briskly away. Rodney had not heard the older one utter a word, but he had a feeling that the eyes hidden behind those tinted glasses had been taking everything in. Some instinct restrained him from moving until the men had vanished round the bend, so they wouldn't realise that he and Sheila had any connection with Mr Drake.

"That was the boss's son," explained the cellarman. "Very different from his father – and from his sister." The disapproval in his voice was evident.

"He wouldn't go into the firm to help Mr Peblow," Sheila added. "It's such an old family business – the Peblows have been here since the year dot. Dad says it would have broken Mr Peblow's heart if there'd been no one to carry on after him. Luckily Miss Jenny said *she'd* come in — "

"She's worth ten of Master Simon!" said Mr Drake disgustedly. "Yet he's always running her down. Says it's no trade for a woman, and what can a girl know about wine. Well, she's learnt all her father can teach her – and a bit more. Fair's fair, I always say."

Sheila's father didn't expect every son to follow the family trade. If Simon didn't fancy the wine business he'd every right to choose a career of his own. But not to stand in his sister's way if she was prepared to help her old dad.

"Course, he don't care a damn about the business, Rodney. It's my belief he'd like Mr Peblow to sell up now—"

"But what about *you*?" cried Sheila in horror. "Your job!"

"I reckon that young fellow wouldn't worry his head much about the staff," he said grimly. "And you needn't, either, my girl," he added reassuringly. "He'll never talk Mr Peblow into selling up. Peblow's is as sound as the rock it stands on."

"What line did Mr Simon go in for?" Rodney asked.

"There you have me, Rodney. I don't rightly know. Deals and schemes of all sorts. He's never settled. And he's never made his fortune, that's for sure. When I seen him just now I thought he was looking for his dad, to touch him for money again." He stopped abruptly. "But I shouldn't gossip about my boss's family affairs. Bad for ship's discipline, as we used to say."

For the rest of the walk home they talked about the cellars and others he knew about in different corners of the inner city. Several pubs had them. The Salutation and the Lion and the Bell. And the famous old Trip to Jerusalem at the base of the Castle Rock. Some had been found beneath shops and offices.

"I believe parties can go down them," he said.

"I wonder— " began Sheila.

"Dunno about kids. Might be difficult, specially on licensed premises."

They came to the street corner where they parted. Rodney remembered his manners and thanked Mr Drake. "It was really interesting. Specially that ancient archway – and that letter V!"

"See you at school tomorrow," said Sheila. "It's Mrs Ledbury after break. We've got to think of something for her blessed project."

23

"I've got an idea for that," he said.

"Such as what?"

"Why not take the caves and cellars under the town?"

He was gratified by her prompt response. "What a super idea, Rod!"

"I do sometimes have 'em," he said modestly.

Chapter Four

In Mrs Ledbury's lesson next day everything went to plan.

Sheila had tackled Debby earlier and, as expected, found her quite agreeable. "Caves? Fine with me," said the black girl. "Might even be a bit spooky! We got to choose *something*, or she'll set us something dead boring."

Rodney meanwhile was working on Kanshi Ram. Kanshi was good at drawing maps and diagrams. "You'd be real useful, Kanshi. She'll expect illustrations. We could have scale plans of the layout. Mathematical!"

"I see scope," said Kanshi cautiously. His dark eyes gleamed. "If you want to do these caves, Rodney, OK by me."

Mrs Ledbury was thankful that one group had come along with a clear idea of their own. She had enough to do, sorting out the rest of the class. Half of them wanted to do the Robin Hood legend. She made them draw lots for it. The rest were gradually steered or bullied into taking other themes – the siege of the castle by the Cavaliers, how the town council had worked in bygone centuries, or the development of the different local industries.

By the time the bell rang she was slightly tetchy, but she had got them all slotted into a list of suitable projects. "And the best of luck," she concluded with relief, "and don't forget to use the public library." Great on the public library, Mrs Ledbury was.

Sheila certainly wouldn't have forgotten it. But it took a day or two before she could marshall all her group together. When they filed into the quiet upstairs department labelled *LOCAL STUDIES* it was clear from the face of the man at the enquiry desk that he had already been visited by other members of their class.

"You don't have to tell me, you're doing a project," he said wearily. "What's yours? Robin Hood? Lacemaking – or the Reform Riots?"

He seemed quite nice, actually. His sandy eyebrows were comically unkempt, and the green eyes under them had a twinkle.

"Please," said Sheila, "have you anything about the caves under the town centre?"

"The caves? Makes a change, anyhow. No, you won't believe this, but in all these books — " he waved a freckled hand round the crowded shelves that went up to the ceiling – "nobody's got around to writing a book on *them*."

"Oh … " Sheila looked at her friends and they looked back at her, equally crestfallen. This was a setback.

"It's only lately they've been studied in a systematic way," the librarian explained. "They keep opening up new ones. Just a moment, though — "

He limped across to a shelf on the far wall. He came back with a slim booklet. "There's this, got out by the Civic Society." He flicked the pages. There were photographs, and a plan marking caves, and the sites of others that had been bulldozed by modern builders.

There were dozens of symbols peppering the street plan of the inner city.

"Can we take this home?" asked Rodney.

"This is a *reference* department," said the man in a shocked tone, as though Rodney had been asking to borrow a body from a cemetery. "You must sit down at one of these tables. Make notes. Or use the photocopier. But it's ten pence a sheet, and the photographs won't come out."

Sheila looked at her colleagues. Their faces were sufficient answer. No one had budgeted for expenses.

She sat down and opened her notebook. The boys sat on either side of her. Debby wasn't one to sit down much. She sort of hovered, fidgeting, and then drifted off to explore the shelves for herself.

"Look at this!" cried Rodney. "Underground chapel – dating right back to 1250!"

"Demolished now," said Sheila, "covered by a petrol filling-station. What a shame!"

"What does this mean," Kanshi asked, "a malt kiln?"

No one was sure, but a caption explained. It was a deep circular pit, like an immense bowl, cut down into the rock. A slow fire would have burned in the bottom of it, and barley would have been spread over a grille above, to be heated and turned into malt for ale.

Kanshi started making a methodical list of all the purposes for which the caves had once been used.

Malting
Brewing
Tanning
Storage (barley, salted meat, ale, wine, herrings)
Wagon-making

"Why should they make *wagons* underground?" said Rodney.

"Why indeed?" said a voice over their shoulders. It was not Debby hovering, but the lame librarian.

"They're so *big*," said Rodney.

"I'm glad to see you've grasped the first rule of the intelligent researcher – he must ask intelligent questions." The librarian's tone was now positively amiable.

"And what is the answer to this one, sir?" enquired Kanshi.

"Do you think I should tell you, just like that? Your teacher expects you to find the answers for yourselves."

"She told us to come here," said Sheila. "I thought the library was supposed to help us."

"To help, yes, but not hand everything to you on a plate. Still, I think I might ask *you* another question. When you see old buildings in the city pulled down, and new ones built, why are the new ones so often these great ugly blocks? Always much higher?"

"That's obvious," said Rodney scornfully. "My dad says, they build as high as the planners will let them. Space is valuable."

"And wasn't it in the Middle Ages?"

"Not like nowadays." Sheila sprang to support her friend. "There weren't so many people. They'd room to spread out."

"Had they? In *this* town?"

Talking to this odd man was like a constant struggle with a tangle of knotted string. One question after another. Why couldn't he just tell them? But of course he was on Mrs Ledbury's side.

It took about five minutes to get it out of him – or rather for *him* to draw it out of *them*. There had been a wall round the medieval town. Outside it lay the common fields, where every citizen could graze his animals and no one could build. By 1845 the town had become the unhealthiest, most overcrowded place in England. Only then was the law changed so that it could spread beyond its ancient boundaries.

Why couldn't people solve their space problem by building higher? "They hadn't modern methods and materials," said Rodney. "Steel girders and all that."

They had built downwards instead, excavating deep cellars in the easy sandstone or enlarging natural caves. They had been forced to use them sometimes for trades they would normally have practised on the surface.

When Kanshi had finished his list Sheila took over the brochure. "I spotted some contemporary quotes!"

"What on earth are they?" asked Debby.

"Things people wrote at the time. *You* know. Mrs Ledbury's mad on them. They're evidence."

Sheila scribbled, muttering excitedly. "This says the town was *'famed all over England'* for its ale. Someone called Dr Deering, 1751." She noted the date with care. "And it wasn't just because they had the best barley, but *'they have also the best, coolest and deepest rock cellars to store their liquor in, many being 20, 24 to 26 steps, nay in some places there are cellars within cellars deeper and deeper in the rock.'*"

"Like the blocked-up one at Peblow's," said Rodney. He kept on thinking about that tantalising little mystery.

Sheila was copying another paragraph: *"Att ye Crown*

Inn is a cellar of 60 stepps down, all in ye rock, like arch worke over your head; in ye cellar, I drank good ale." That was by a lady, Celia Fiennes, 1697. Sheila kept the odd spellings. If Mrs Ledbury thought they were *her* mistakes the laugh would be against her.

The librarian drifted back. "You seem to be getting on all right," he said encouragingly. "What made you choose the caves in the first place?"

They told him about the Mortimer's Hole trip, and then the visit to the wine cellars. "You don't know what this letter V would stand for?" Rodney asked.

"Hm … It might be a mason's mark."

"What is that?" Kanshi enquired.

"The master mason was very important in the old days. When a job was finished he signed it with his personal mark, cut into the stone. But that would usually be on some major construction, a cathedral tower, say. Hardly for a bit of walling."

"P'raps it does just mean number five cellar," said Rodney. But he was still faintly dissatisfied.

It was time to go home. They had made a start on the project. Tomorrow they would visit some caves that were open to the public.

"Let me know if I can help you in any other way," said the librarian. "If you don't find me on the desk ask one of the young ladies to tell me."

"Who do we ask for?" said Sheila.

"Oh, my name? Mr Blasterman."

Debby giggled. Rodney turned away hastily.

"Yes, it is a funny name, I know," said the librarian. "I got used to jokes about it in the Air Force."

"It's a very unusual name," said Rodney. He looked

with interest, and with new respect, at the sandy-haired man behind the enquiry desk. The Air Force! So he wasn't just an old bookworm. Maybe he limped because he'd been wounded or been in a crash.

"It was originally 'Alabasterman', then 'Alablaster-man', and then it got shortened. It meant a stone carver – you know, alabaster. The main quarries for it were in this part of the country, and the town became a centre for the trade. The carvings were exported to places as far away as Italy and Spain, even Iceland. So there were dozens of 'alabastermen' here, and I must be descended from one of them."

"So it's just a name – like Baker or Butcher or Carpenter?" said Sheila. "But much more unusual," she added politely. "And interesting about the alabaster, and the town once being so famous for it."

"A pity you didn't choose it for your project. I *could* have told you a few things about that."

Or asked us a lot of questions, thought Rodney, but he was beginning to see the point of the method. It taught you to ask yourself questions, and gradually ferret out the truth. As a detective would.

The next morning they met in the town centre and joined a party going down some caves under the offices of a building society. The lady guiding them looked amused at their pencils and notebooks, but when she saw that they were seriously interested she proved very helpful.

There was a glass-fronted recess in the rock displaying fragments of pottery and a broken flagon that had been stuck together. "These finds date from about 1270," she said.

There was a round hole in the floor, covered by a modern iron grating, with a shaft vanishing into the darkness. "This was the well," she told them. "Many of the caves had deep wells."

"Is this another one, miss?" Kanshi called from the next cellar.

"No, the experts tell us it was a garderobe."

Kanshi wanted to know what a "garderobe" was, and some of the grown ups twittered knowingly. "I think it was a toilet," whispered Sheila. Rodney told him, more loudly, "It was the bog, you fool."

After this tour they took a short cut across the churchyard to get a Coke in the shopping centre. As they clattered over the flagstones round the ancient parish church Kanshi let out a cry. "Just a moment, Rod! Take a look at this."

He was pointing to the outer wall of the ornate stone porch they were passing.

Rodney stared. "It's that V," he said.

Chapter Five

"Wonder if the same man did it," said Debby.

"You bet he did," said Rodney. "It's one of those masons' marks, like what the man at the library — "

"If only we could find out when this was done," Kanshi interrupted, "we'd know when he did the wall in the cellar. To within a few years, anyhow."

"We could ask that nice Mr Blasterman," said Debby.

"He'd be even nicer," Sheila suggested, "if we tried to find out for ourselves first. They often have leaflets in a church, on a table just inside."

Rodney was in the porch like lightning, raising the heavy latch. The immense door squeaked back. They tiptoed into the gloom. "There!" whispered Rodney in triumph.

He snatched a leaflet from the top of a pile. It gave a potted history of the building, with dates and architectural styles.

The porch had been added in 1538, a good example of very late Gothic. *"There were originally some fine alabaster statuettes inside it, above the door, carved by local craftsmen. These vanished in the general destruction of religious images during the reign of Edward VI."*

"Mr Blasterman wouldn't have liked that," said Rodney.

They went out into the porch and looked up. Sure

enough, there were three empty niches just above the doorway, where the little figures would have been well sheltered from the weather.

Sheila stood silent, picturing the scene. Shocked townspeople, too scared to protest, watching while grim-faced Puritan fanatics pulled down the beautifully carved images and savagely smashed them up with hammers. She remembered a lesson on that wild period of religious conflict, the executions, the burnings at the stake …

"Let's go to the library," said Rodney. He had kept the leaflet as it was free. So, after quickly gulping a Coke in the shopping centre, they hurried off to consult Mr Blasterman.

He shushed them sternly when they burst in upon the calm of his department. But his welcome grew warmer when he saw the leaflet.

"Now you're getting somewhere. The same V, carved on the porch? That gives you an approximate date."

"It does not say who built the porch," said Kanshi, "this mysterious V, who also walled up the cave at Peblow's."

Mr Blasterman made light of that difficulty. "Leaflets can't cover every detail. But you'd be amazed what details *are* still on record somewhere, if you know where to look." He limped across to a shelf of dusty-looking volumes and pulled out a history of the parish church. "Here," he said, turning the pages, "the master mason was Matthew Venner."

"So it was V for Venner!" cried Debby.

"You *are* bright," said Rodney crushingly. He craned forward. "It even says what he was *paid*."

Mr Blasterman smiled. "That's usually why these names get recorded."

"Not much for a job that size! My dad wouldn't look at it."

"Money was worth more in the sixteenth century." Mr Blasterman turned the page. "It so happens that this ties up with my own study of the 'alabastermen'. Listen to this: *'The three niches above the door originally held statues of the Madonna and Child, John the Baptist, and the Apostle Peter, commissioned from Thomas Barwell, a leading stone carver in the town, but these disappeared in the wholesale destruction of 1550.'* It's quite rare to get the names of these craftsmen, although their work went all over Europe."

Rodney was not interested in Thomas Barwell. The great thing was they had now established that the V in the wine cellar stood for that Matthew Venner who had built the church porch in 1538. So the archway had been blocked up somewhere about that time, during Venner's working life.

No one in the world but themselves knew this. It was hardly a world-shaking fact, but Mrs Ledbury said that the tiniest scrap of fresh knowledge could be important. Would any other group in the class show up a project with anything that hadn't been cribbed straight from a book?

"Can you tell us anything else about Venner?" he asked.

"Or where we could find out?" said Sheila tactfully.

"The only place where you could look would be in my private notes on the alabastermen – and I'm not letting you loose there! I've a card index of a thousand references —"

36

Debby gasped in admiration.

"I don't bother with masons in the ordinary way – they're not in my field of research. But I do have a card for Venner, because he was a friend of Barwell and worked with him." Mr Blasterman disappeared to his cubbyhole at the back, and returned holding a neatly written index card. "Not much, I'm afraid. But copy it down by all means."

Sheila did so. Venner had been born in the town and baptised on July 11th, 1510. There was a list of the main buildings he had worked on. He had died on September 10th, 1552, leaving a widow and two daughters. There was a summary of his will, naming as executor *"my good friend, Thomas Barwell, master carver in alabaster, of this town"*. The librarian had underlined these words in red.

It was not very helpful. They now knew a little about the man who had walled up the archway, but not why he had been asked to do so, or what, if anything, lay behind it. It must have been done in the reign of Henry VIII or his son, Edward VI. Venner had died before Mary became Queen.

In the library's entrance hall the four friends conferred before separating to their homes.

All agreed that Peblow's cellars should be specially featured in their project. They were not spectacular, not even mentioned in the brochure, but for that reason Mrs Ledbury might give them extra credit for finding fresh material. The Pillar Cave *was* rather like another discovered under the city, dating from 1270. And the archway must be pretty ancient if it had been walled up by 1552.

Kanshi would draw a plan, if Mr Peblow would let him, with the complete layout of the cellars. He would sketch the archway, clearly showing the carved V. Mr Peblow might not want the whole gang of them running round on his premises, so Sheila would just take Kanshi along and explain why they were asking this favour.

That evening her father felt sure that it would be all right. "I'll mention it to the boss in the morning," he promised, "but he'll like it best if you come and ask him yourselves."

Early on the following afternoon she took Kanshi along to Gillyflower Hill. Young Liz behind the counter knew her and smiled a welcome. Being busy serving a customer she waved them through to Mr Peblow's office.

It was not the first time that Sheila had visited this inner sanctum. The cosy carpeted room, with its old-fashioned rolltop desk and cheerful gas fire, did not in any way intimidate her. Nor did little Mr Peblow himself, with his neat moustache and quiff of silvered hair, his countrified tweed suit and the old spaniel that dozed in the corner.

Only today Mr Peblow was not to be seen. The spaniel was, but after a non-committal growl closed its eyes again. Miss Jenny, however, was there, standing beside her typing table. She held an open bottle of wine in one hand and a glass in the other, and wore an expression of intense concentration. She raised the glass in greeting, but did not utter a word. The muscles were moving round her tightly closed lips. Then she turned, bent her head, and spat a mouthful of red wine into a pail standing discreetly behind her chair.

Kanshi stood petrified with amazement. Sheila was not so puzzled, especially when Miss Jenny scribbled something on her writing pad, and then faced them with a smile.

"Sorry about that! I couldn't speak with my mouth full. If wine merchants swallowed all the wine they had to taste they'd soon be under the table."

Sheila liked Miss Jenny. She was brisk and businesslike, always rather severely tailored in the office, but good looking. "Pretty as a picture," Sheila's father summed her up, "but firm as the frame!" She had to be in the liquor trade.

Sheila came up against that firmness as soon as she began to explain their mission.

"I don't think it's at all possible this afternoon, Sheila. Your father's up to his eyes, getting the orders sent out. If you and your friend are stretching tape measures everywhere – no, I'm afraid you'll have to come another day."

Miss Jenny was not a person to argue with. Fortunately, at that moment, Mr Peblow himself came bustling in. The spaniel sprang to life in the hope of a walk.

"I'm just off, Jenny. Ah, Sheila! Your father mentioned something this morning. I told him it would be quite all right. Do go ahead."

"I don't think it's very convenient at the moment," said Miss Jenny crisply. "Sam's busy down there — "

"Oh, they won't get in his way. Will you, Sheila?"

Miss Jenny shrugged her shoulders, and, before the permission could be withdrawn, Sheila stammered their thanks and got Kanshi out of the office, and into the yard.

Joe, the vanman, was loading twelve-bottle cartons

which came rumbling up in the lift. Down below, they found Sheila's father and his assistant sending up the cartons as they checked them on the invoices. One dozen burgundy, one mixed dozen of French white wines … Kanshi and Sheila squeezed past and set to work. Very soon Kanshi had got his ground plan and all the dimensions.

There was nothing more that Sheila could do to help. They needed only a drawing of the Pillar Cave and another of the archway. Kanshi would get on better by himself.

She found Miss Jenny in the yard, giving some instructions to the vanman. She thanked her and made for the gate, just as a young man came hurrying in. It was the one she had seen on Sunday morning, Miss Jenny's brother.

"Simon!" said Miss Jenny coldly. "Quite a stranger. I'm afraid Father's just gone out."

"That's all right. I didn't want to see him."

"You don't surprise me. But do you actually want to see *me*?"

"Yes, as a matter of fact, I do. Privately."

"Go into the office then – if you remember the way! I'll be with you in a minute."

Chapter Six

Meanwhile, far below, Kanshi was sketching the archway. He had brought a powerful electric torch which would stand on the floor and throw a circle of brilliant light upon his subject.

It was quiet now down here. The goods lift had ceased to travel up and down. Sam Drake had sent his assistant upstairs and was about to follow him. Kanshi would be left alone in this eerie gloom, but he was too intent upon his task to mind that.

The silence was suddenly broken by the vibrant ring of an old-fashioned telephone, distant but remarkably distinct.

Sam Drake had just come into the cellar for a special bottle of vintage port. His exclamation of surprise startled Kanshi more than the telephone.

"Well, I never heard that before – not down here! Not in all the years I've been here." Sheila's father sounded incredulous. "That's in the office upstairs." The ringing ceased and Miss Jenny's voice answered, the words too faint to be audible.

"It is strange in caves," said Kanshi. "There are peculiar sound effects. Water can wear a passage through the rock — "

"True enough. Specially in sandstone."

"It might conduct the sound, like a speaking tube."

"I s'pose it might, lad. But why haven't I ever noticed

it before? The hours I've spent in these cellars!"

Kanshi considered. "Perhaps it is only in this corner? Sheila says there were always wine racks in front of the archway. Perhaps — " He shone his torch on the roof of the cave. It was rough, grooved and fissured with shadowy recesses. "Yes, see, Mr Drake! There is a hole, I think! If it was worn by water it may start from near the surface."

"That probably explains it. Smart lad! Got a head on your shoulders." The cellarman departed with the bottle he had come for, and his footsteps faded up the stairs.

Kanshi continued happily with his sketch. This was something he was good at. Mrs Ledbury would be pleased.

From far overhead floated the murmur of Miss Jenny's voice, taking down an order it seemed, for he caught the phrase, "Delivery tomorrow, without fail – goodbye." After a brief silence a man's voice spoke, louder and much clearer.

"Come over here, Jenny, and sit down. And remember, this is still just between us."

"I don't like having secrets from Father."

Miss Jenny's voice was louder now. She had obviously crossed the room and was now just above the place from which the sound was somehow transmitted to the cave below.

"We'll tell him, all in good time," said the man impatiently. "We'll need his signature. But we've got to talk first. He's an obstinate old fool — "

"If that's how you're going to talk about Father — "

"Cool down, girl! There's big money at stake. For you as well as me. When the old man pops off — "

42

"Simon!"

"He can't live for ever. When he goes, we'll be sharing fifty–fifty. But how much?"

"I don't want to think about it."

"You must. Suppose he died tomorrow, what would he leave? An old-fashioned little business – what would it fetch if it was put up for sale?"

"Why should it be?" Her anger vibrated through the narrow passage in the rock.

Simon's answer was cold and full of menace. "Because I'd want my share in cash – and quick. You couldn't buy me out. You'd have to agree. We'd sell it and split the proceeds."

"Never! Father would turn in his grave."

Kanshi realised that he was eavesdropping, but he had not meant to. He could not abandon his sketch unfinished and go away. His pencil worked on, but he could not close his ears to the argument that filtered down to him from the office above.

Miss Jenny's brother was explaining what a dazzling opportunity had been suddenly laid before them. A big property company was buying up all these decrepit old buildings on Gillyflower Hill. They would be demolished and a mammoth office block erected on the site. The company would pay almost anything to get possession of Peblow's and the neighbouring buildings – price was no object, for their scheme would bring immense profits.

Miss Jenny sounded horrified. "An office block? One of those hideous eyesores? Destroy one of the last corners of the town with a bit of character! And wipe out Peblow's, after the family's traded here for two hundred years! You must be crazy. Father would never agree."

"He will, if *you* work on him. You were always his favourite."

"Well, I won't. They can leave Peblow's out of their ghastly scheme."

"They can't. They must have this whole slice of land. They can't go ahead with their plan unless every owner agrees to sell."

"Splendid! Then we can stop it. Father doesn't want their money, however much they offer. And I wouldn't ask him."

"Then I'll have to handle him myself. And I shall, don't worry." Again the man's voice was full of threat. "I shall make him see sense. Nothing you can say will stop me."

"You're a devil, Simon. You always have been. You'd stick at nothing."

"Well, as long as you remember that, dear sister!" The man's voice faded as he moved away. A door shut. Whatever Miss Jenny's thoughts she did not speak them aloud.

Kanshi also was very thoughtful as he completed his task in the cellars. He was taking in the full implications of the conversation he had overheard.

Although his own father was a taxi driver he came of a business family. Ever since he could remember, he had heard constant talk of deals, investment in shops or lodging houses, land values and profits. He was not shocked by Simon Peblow's eagerness to sell this old building for a high price. What shocked him was that Simon should speak so contemptuously of his father and look forward to inheriting his money when he died.

44

It was not the way that Kanshi had been brought up to regard his elders.

As he walked away down Gillyflower Hill another thought struck him, more worrying than his fears for the kindly old wine merchant and his daughter. Miss Jenny had said that Peblow's would be "wiped out". And so it would be if this development scheme went through. The shabby, yet somehow gracious, old building would be bulldozed out of existence, and replaced by a soaring cliff of concrete offices. With the former building would go the business – and with that would go Mr Drake's job.

Where, at his age, would he find another? Kanshi realised with dismay that even his friend Sheila was threatened by what he had just learnt.

Chapter Seven

That same afternoon Rodney had agreed, rather reluctantly, to do his stint of research at the library.

He would have been happier going round some more cave cellars. Leafing through old books was a tedious and mainly fruitless task, especially when there was no index. Mr Blasterman would only throw out a few hints and suggestions.

Another cause for irritation was being paired with Debby. Rodney liked her well enough – she was quick witted, she was fun – but at historical research she was a dead loss. Still, she had to be worked into the project. Luckily she wrote a clear, painstaking hand, much better than his own impatient scrawl. When he did come upon some scrap of information in a book, she would copy it down without complaint.

One quote should gladden their teacher's heart. Enemy soldiers had looted the town in 1140. A merchant had tricked a gang of them into believing that his wealth was hidden in the cave cellar beneath his house. They had all rushed down the steps, he had barred the door after them, and had then set fire to the house.

"Better have this in full," said Rodney.

So Debby, tongue between shining teeth with intense concentration, copied the whole passage to the end. *"So all the thieves, to the number of thirty, were burnt; and by reason of this fire all the town was set in flames."*

Mr Blasterman came over. "Ah, you've spotted this!"

"It's about all we *have* found," grumbled Rodney.

"Things turn up in the most unlikely places. Don't despair." The librarian went off to his cubbyhole and returned with a shabby volume. "Here's an example. I picked this up on my holidays. You know my special interest, our local alabaster carvers? You'd hardly expect to find anything about them in this." He pointed to the faded gold title.

"*Commercial Correspondence of Tudor London,*" read Debby.

He turned the pages. The book was a collection of letters, numbered and dated, with footnotes. They were addressed to various London merchants or their customers in the sixteenth century, concerning orders and shipments. Some mentioned the risk of a war or the spread of plague in Genoa, but mostly they looked deadly dull.

Rodney and Debby murmured politely, but were not impressed.

"I glanced at the index," said Mr Blasterman, "and my luck was in. Remember Thomas Barwell?"

Rodney did. "The bloke who carved statues for the porch?"

"Yes. Several of his letters are here, kept by the merchant who handled his foreign commissions." Mr Blasterman found the section concerned. The letters were spread over the years and looked no more exciting than the rest of the volume. They were all about altarpieces and Madonnas and heads of John the Baptist, with prices and dates of delivery. A few personal passages, enquiring after each other's

47

families, showed that the merchant and the master carver were close friends.

"This bit mystified me." Mr Blasterman laid his finger on the page. Rodney read: *"I thank you most heartily for the warning and have followed your counsel. It were best not to confide details in a letter, but I can set your mind at rest. Unless Joshua blow his trumpet again, the secret will be safe. It is fit that a great angel should shelter smaller angels under his wing."*

For the first time Rodney's interest was aroused. "Sounds like a code. They haven't the letter the merchant wrote?"

"Alas, no. Most of this correspondence is one way only. It was the merchants who filed the letters they received."

A lady was drumming her fingers impatiently on the enquiry desk. The librarian hurried over to her.

Rodney studied the letter again. There was a story here. "Make us a copy of this," he instructed Debby.

"It's nothing to do with caves."

"Never mind. Copy it just the same."

"OK. Whatever you say."

His brows puckered as she wrote. He could not see how this quote would fit into their project. Mrs Ledbury would say "irrelevant", a favourite word of hers. But – bother the project! Barwell's enigmatic words suggested a "secret" at which he dared only hint to his friend.

"You've left out the date," he told Debby severely.

"Does it matter?" Even the easy-going Debby verged on revolt.

"You never know. April the tenth, 1550."

They had done enough for today. Clearly Mr Blasterman would be occupied with the impatient lady for some time. Rodney went to the desk and laid the book silently under his eye. The librarian smiled and nodded, the lady continued her nonstop harangue. Rodney and Debby melted away.

The quartet gathered after tea in the garden shed at Rodney's. Kanshi displayed his sketches. "Only rough," he said, "but when I've worked on them — "

"They'll be super," said Sheila.

Kanshi seemed to have something else on his mind, but Rodney was full 'of the mystery in the master carver's letter.

"I can't see how it fits into the project," said Sheila.

"Maybe not, but it's a sight more interesting than any mouldy project. If only we could crack the code! This stuff about angels – 'It is fit that a great angel should shelter smaller angels' – what's that supposed to mean?"

Kanshi asked what exactly an angel was. They did not have them in his religion. The others explained but fell into an argument as to whether an angel was male or female. It was settled only when Rodney ran indoors for the dictionary. An angel could be either.

But – what was far more interesting – in 1550 an angel was also a gold coin. Rodney let out a triumphant yell.

"You *see*? This could be something! Hidden treasure!"

His enthusiasm infected them all. "How much was it worth, this coin?" asked Kanshi.

The dictionary said, a third or two-thirds of a pound. But they all knew how money values had altered over four centuries. A bag of 1550 angels, maybe the life savings of a prosperous craftsman, would have increased vastly.

"If it was still there," said Kanshi sensibly. "But probably this Barwell dug it up again, as soon as the scare had passed over, whatever it was." Anyhow, he relentlessly pointed out, even if there was a hoard of golden angels still lying in a hiding place, the letter gave no clue as to their whereabouts.

Rodney looked deflated. Kanshi seized his opening to tell them of the conversation he had overheard in the cellar.

"I did not mean to listen, but how could I help it?"

"You couldn't," said Sheila. She had gone very white. "But this is awful. I wonder if Dad knows. He could be out of work! I don't know what he'd *do*."

Chapter Eight

For the next few days Sheila was so worried that she could hardly set her mind to the school project.

She longed to ask her father if he knew about the plan that threatened Gillyflower Hill. But it would mean reporting what Kanshi had overheard. Dad would go up in smoke. Kanshi would never be allowed in the cellars again. She herself might be banned from the premises. They'd been let in as a special favour, for their project, not to eavesdrop on people's private affairs.

Mum noticed her glum look and asked if anything was bothering her. Sheila said "no". She realised that she was not the only worried member of the family. Dad wasn't his usual cheery self. Mum was watching *him* now, and beginning in turn to look depressed. Only Kevin, forever tinkering with his blessed motorbike outside, had no care in the world beyond the state of its engine.

Mum and Dad had long low-voiced discussions, breaking off suddenly if Sheila entered the room. She guessed that they were talking about Peblow's. But she wasn't going to listen behind doors. They couldn't accuse *her* of eavesdropping.

At last they gave her an opening. She was sitting quietly with a book when they came in, too deep in talk to notice that she was there. Mum was saying, "You'd get another job, Sam, I'm sure you would — "

"At *my* age? With all this unemployment?"

Sheila had never heard her father so bitter. "What's happened, Dad?" she said. "You've never lost your *job?*"

"Might as well tell her," said Mum grimly. "If it happens, she'll have to know."

Dad made an effort. "Don't worry, Sheila. May be a false alarm." He slumped into his easy chair.

"But tell me – please," she begged.

"It's that no-good son of poor Mr Peblow's," said Mum.

"He's been in and out, the last few days," Dad explained. "On at his father to sell out to some big company. They want to build some glass and concrete monstrosity — "

"Peblow's!" said Mum. "How can he even consider it?"

"I've told you, love. It's the sort of offer he can't refuse. Or so young Simon tells him."

"Horrible creature! No thought but money, money!"

"Let's face it." Dad was a fair-minded man. "For him this might be a big chance. He's always needing cash for some deal or other. His father's money is locked up in the business and he'll get none till his father dies. Then the business will be sold fast enough, mark my words – Simon will twist Miss Jenny's arm till she has to agree. But he wants some cash *now*, and he reckons he could have it if the boss would accept this offer."

"How awful!" said Sheila. It was just as Kanshi had explained it.

"They'd all be out of jobs!" Mum sounded furious. "Even Miss Jenny – and she's set her heart on continuing the firm when the old man retires. Simon may not care twopence about you and the others – but to do this to his own sister! And what's Mr Peblow himself thinking of? His own daughter! Who's worked her fingers to the bone — "

"He's always wanted to treat them both alike. And he may wonder if it wouldn't be the best for *her* in the long run. No joke for her, running the business with Simon owning a half share, and not being able to buy him out. Awkward."

"I should think so – with a brother like that!"

"Well, love, we'll have to see. The boss hasn't decided yet. He's had a word with me – which I appreciated – but I mustn't say more at the moment."

"I do hope it works out," said Sheila. But her heart was heavy.

She did not feel free to discuss things with her friends. When she met them she tried to throw herself into the project, but her old enthusiasm had gone. They had a few caves to visit, one or two items to research at the library, but they had now gathered most of the available information. The Easter Bank Holiday weekend was near. After that, they must get their fair copy made before term began.

Rodney had really taken over the leadership. But his interest had been diverted by Barwell's mysterious letter to the London merchant in 1550. He niggled away at its coded phrases, convinced that some treasure had lain undiscovered until the present day.

Mr Blasterman doubted that theory. "Barwell never had any great fortune. Stone carvers wouldn't – and their business was ruined by the Protestant campaign against religious images. I have his will, May 1553

– he didn't long outlive Venner. He left very little."

"That only proves he hadn't dug up his gold again!"

"But it certainly doesn't prove that he ever had any."

Even Rodney could not argue with Mr Blasterman on his own subject. But later, with his friends gathered in the garden shed, he went over the letter for the twentieth time.

"Who's this Joshua?" Kanshi demanded.

"Someone in the Bible," said Sheila vaguely.

"He was an Israelite leader," said Debby. "He besieged the city of Jericho. The Lord told them to march round, and blow their trumpets seven times, and shout – and the walls would fall down. So they did, and the walls did fall."

The others goggled at this confident flow of information. But of course Debby and her family were great churchgoers.

"I know – I've heard about it!" cried Rodney. "The walls fell flat. Don't you see what Barwell meant?"

"Frankly, no," said Sheila.

"So long as Joshua's trumpet didn't make the wall fall down — "

"Which wall?"

"The one in Peblow's cellar, idiot! Think," Rodney commanded them all. "Venner built that wall. Venner and Barwell were mates. If Barwell wanted to hide something behind a wall, who would he get to help him? Suppose Barwell's house was on that very spot?"

"No," said Sheila. "Mr Peblow told Dad that there'd been an inn there, going right back to the Middle Ages. But we could ask Mr Blasterman. *He'd* know."

And of course Mr Blasterman did. His notes contained every recorded fact about the master carver. He had lived on the far side of the town.

"But you're right about there being an inn there, where Peblow's stands today. Let me just check ... " He vanished into his cubbyhole. "Ah, yes," he told them a minute later. "It was the Golden Angel."

Rodney's yell of triumph shattered the peace of the library, and several elderly researchers looked up in horrified disgust.

Chapter Nine

Sheila sensed that Mr Blasterman was as excited as Rodney, but was trying to hide it. "I do apologise," he announced to the room in general, adding sternly to Rodney, "we must not disturb other library users. We'll discuss this in my office."

He led them behind the enquiry desk. "Miss Pritchard!" he called. A green-overalled young lady popped out between the filing cabinets like an inquisitive rabbit. "Would you take over for a few minutes?"

His office proved to be a narrow slit of space, a ravine walled by soaring cliffs of bookcases. Mr Blasterman sat down at a littered table and waved Sheila to the only other chair. Debby and the boys stood on what scanty floor space remained.

The librarian smiled up at Rodney, his show of sternness gone. "You've solved part of my puzzle for me. It was staring me in the face all the time!"

"The great angel, sir?"

"Of course. *'It is fit that a great angel — '*"

" — *'should shelter smaller angels under his wing,'*" broke in Sheila. She too knew the mysterious letter word for word.

"The treasure could still be at Peblow's!" cried Rodney.

"You've a bee in your bonnet about treasure," said Mr

Blasterman. "I don't believe in it myself. Barwell wasn't likely to have had any."

"He only mentioned a 'secret'," Kanshi pointed out.

"Exactly. We mustn't jump to conclusions. 'Smaller angels' don't have to mean coins. I doubt if we'll ever know what the secret was, but we'll go on trying. You've made one interesting discovery – this link with the inn. And 'Joshua's trumpet' would certainly tie up with that blocked-up archway. I'm beginning to feel like Rodney – I'd give a lot to know what lies behind it."

"I wonder if Mr Peblow — " Sheila began. But she remembered the wine merchant's present anxieties. Could they possibly bother him just now? She could not say this to Mr Blasterman, she had to let him go ahead. He clearly thought it was time for an adult to take over. This was becoming more than a school project.

"I'm sure Mr Peblow would be reasonable," he said, "if approached in the proper way. A scientific investigation. Under expert supervision. Perhaps by the Archaeological Society — "

Rodney's face was a picture of dismay. Sheila felt a surge of sympathy. After all, it was his curiosity that had started everything. Now that the investigation was getting really exciting, it was to become a grown ups' affair. She plucked up her courage and said, "We could watch, though – couldn't we?"

The librarian stared at her, as if he was already forgetting the vital part they had played. "I don't know what the archaeologists would say. A lot of children standing round. There's not much space there, I imagine."

"Like in your office," said Rodney with a scowl.

"If it hadn't been for my dad working there," Sheila said hurriedly, "we'd never have seen the mason's mark. And if Rod hadn't mentioned it to *you* — "

"Ye-es. I see how you feel, my dear. You young people deserve most of the credit."

"Great," said Rodney. "So long as we don't get pushed out."

"You shan't be." Mr Blasterman checked Peblow's number, lifted the telephone, and pressed the buttons. Faintly they heard a woman's voice answer.

"This is Adrian Blasterman, Miss Peblow. I wondered if I could speak to Mr Peblow — " He paused and blinked. Sheila could tell that the reaction at the other end had been sharp and suspicious. "No, no," he went on, "I'm nothing to do with a development company – I'm speaking from the City Library … If I might come over at his convenience … Oh, yes, I appreciate he is a busy man … But yes, indeed, if I might explain to *you*? An old archway in your cellars … In half an hour? Thank you, Miss Peblow."

He put down the telephone and mopped his brow. "A very *businesslike* lady! Somewhat alarming."

"She's quite sweet really," Sheila assured him.

"She was certainly more cordial when I said that I was not a development company. Well, we shall see."

Limping up Gillyflower Hill a little later, Mr Blasterman nerved himself for the encounter. Old Peblow he knew by sight, but not his daughter. She sounded a bit of a dragon. He wondered what she'd be like – he'd never met a lady wine merchant.

He had always been fond of Gillyflower Hill. It was full of character. Once it had been a fashionable area for the gentry, even for a lord or two. There were still some fine doorways with fanlights and canopies, tall Georgian windows ranged between pillars and pilasters, and some splendid surviving iron railings. The old magnificence was flaked and faded, but the atmosphere lingered like some elegant ghost. It would be a sad loss if Gillyflower Hill were ever swept away.

Peblow's, despite a shop front of later date, had kept much of the dignity of that earlier age. The old inn, he knew, had been demolished in sixteen-something, and replaced by the present building.

He was pleasantly surprised when Miss Peblow proved to be quite young – perhaps ten years younger than himself, and he after all (though his friends teased him as "an old bachelor") was only forty. Businesslike she certainly was.

"What's this about the archway?" she demanded briskly.

He explained, playing down Rodney's wild idea of treasure. "You know what young people are. I doubt myself if anything of value is hidden behind the wall. If it were, it would belong to your father. He *is* the owner of the building?"

A shadow passed across her face. "Oh, yes. But for how long", she added darkly, "I shouldn't like to say."

She led the way down to the cellars. He stumbled on the uneven rock steps, and she gripped his arm with a cry of concern. "Sorry! These steps are tricky." "I'm all right," he assured her. Inwardly he cursed that plane crash long ago that had left him with this tiresome leg.

They reached the archway. He noticed at once the

mason's mark, V for Venner, which had first set Rodney on the scent.

"Not much to look at," she said. "I suppose it's very old? I don't know much about old things – except vintage wines."

"The arch is probably fourteenth century. The later masonry dates from 1550."

"Goodness! Well, I must get back to the office. Take your time." She was gone, running nimbly up the steps.

He stood silently, surveying the archway. His friends in the Archaeological Society would make light of the job. No need to demolish the later stonework entirely. Just make a gap to squeeze through.

Suddenly he was startled to hear Miss Peblow's voice as clearly as if she were standing at his elbow.

"Oh, you're back, Father! What did the bank manager say?"

Mr Peblow's voice was elderly and weary. "He was very sympathetic. He knows what a wrench it would be for us both — "

"You're telling *me*," she said dourly.

"But a bank manager has to give the best financial advice. There's no doubt in *his* mind. We'll never get such an offer again. For your sake as well as Simon's he says I'd be foolish to turn it down."

"So – you've decided?" Her voice was full of despair.

"Not finally. I'll think it over during this holiday week-end. They couldn't expect me to sign before Tuesday. I'm fighting against this, my dear, as hard as I can – but it does look as though it's something I ought to do."

There was a muffled sound, presumably from the young woman. Then nothing more.

Mr Blasterman did not know how the voices had reached him with such uncanny clarity. He knew only that he had heard things he was not meant to hear. Deeply embarrassed he mounted the cellar steps. He hesitated to disturb Miss Peblow with his thanks, but he met her face to face and was relieved to see that her eyes were dry – and diamond bright.

"My father's back. We could probably settle this now."

The wine merchant was sitting dejectedly at his desk. With her usual matter-of-fact briskness she explained about the archway. "I can see no reason, Father, why they should not have a look."

"No, no, by all means." Mr Peblow's thoughts seemed far away. Suddenly he looked up. "Could it be done quickly?"

"It's only a few hours' work," promised Mr Blasterman.

"Then the sooner the better. After this week-end I might not be in a position to give you authority."

"This week-end?" echoed the librarian, trying to hide his dismay. "But of course – I must see what can be arranged."

Chapter Ten

That evening Sheila found the tension at home almost unbearable.

"Things are coming to a head," said her father gloomily. All Peblow's staff sensed that change was near, perhaps catastrophe. Mr Simon was constantly in and out of the place. He and Miss Jenny were more than ever at daggers drawn. The boss tried desperately to keep the peace between them. He'd been to see his lawyer. This time next week they'd all know the worst.

"You'll get redundancy money," said Kevin soothingly. "If he sells out for a fancy price he'll see you all OK."

"I know he will. But money's not everything – as you young lads seem to think." Worry made Dad snappy. "I don't *want* redundancy. I want to work. I like my job. If Peblow's closes I'll not find another like it."

Next morning the librarian was worried for a different reason.

"Mr Peblow gave his permission," he reported.

"Oh, great!" said Rodney.

"Only there's a snag. The work will have to be done immediately." He hesitated, looking doubtfully round their eager faces. He must know about the property deal, thought Sheila, and he doesn't realise that we do too. Mr Blasterman went on, "We can look behind the wall – frankly I don't think Mr Peblow cares twopence *what* we do."

"What's the snag, sir?" asked Kanshi.

"Time. We need an archaeologist in charge, or valuable historical evidence can be lost for ever."

"Surely the Archaeological Society — " Rodney began.

"I've been telephoning round. I can't find anyone who'll be free this Bank Holiday week-end. They're all off to some Oxford conference. We can't expect anyone to cancel that sort of engagement. We've nothing certain to offer them – just a medieval arch and a bit of Tudor walling — "

"There might be treasure," said Rodney doggedly.

"We've no evidence. These archaeologists — "

Rodney said something rude about archaeologists. The girls giggled. Kanshi said, "Could we not manage without them, sir, if we were very careful? And got grown-ups — "

"My dad would help, I'm sure," said Rodney. "He'd have that wall down in no time. He's a builder. He knows all about it."

"I'm sure he does," said Mr Blasterman, "but it mustn't *be* a quick job. Archaeologists would photograph everything first, then take the wall down slowly, number each stone — "

"*We* can take photographs," said Kanshi. "And number stones."

Debby spoke for the first time. "My pa would come, if he wasn't on that shift. He's awfully strong."

Mr Harker was as huge as his daughter was small.

Sheila's father would naturally be there, as cellarman.

Mr Blasterman's opposition collapsed. He was as

keen to get through that wall as any of them. If they had to put off the job until these professors came back from their conference they might miss their chance for ever.

"Very well," he said, "if your fathers will help — "

"Great!" Rodney almost crowed.

"I want a strict understanding: if we come on anything *really* important and there's the slightest risk of doing damage if we go on, we stop. Like that. And wait for the experts." He looked round sternly. "Is that clear?"

There was a murmur of agreement.

"You too, Rodney?"

Rodney looked mutinous. "S'pose so. We got no choice."

No, we haven't, thought Sheila. Without Mr Blasterman there Miss Jenny wouldn't let us lay a finger on anything.

It was maddening that they had to wait until Easter Monday. Debby's father couldn't manage Good Friday or Sunday, the shop opened Saturday and normal business must not be disrupted. Only the public holiday on Monday suited everybody. That week-end seemed endless.

On Monday morning Sheila and her father were at Gillyflower Hill before nine, to unlock the premises and welcome the others. Mr Peblow had every confidence in Sam Drake. He and his daughter had other matters to think about and could not be bothered with historical investigations.

Sheila and her father hung plastic sheeting over the wine bins, and set out bags and cartons for rubble. They had remembered a pail of whitewash for daubing

numbers on the stones. Chalk might rub off.

Rodney's father brought his tools. Debby's father brought only a pair of immensely powerful arms and a cheerful grin that shone like a moon high above every one else's head. Kanshi carried his last-birthday-present camera, with flash.

"Photos first, I think," he said.

Then Rodney's father looked at the walling and marked out an area that looked easiest to remove without damage, big enough for them to squeeze through.

"Now we number each stone," said Mr Blasterman. Rodney and Sheila seized brushes and began daubing enthusiastically. Kanshi made the sensible suggestion that, if Sheila used only odd numbers and Rodney even, there would be less risk of ending up with two stones bearing the same identification. When they had finished he took another photo as a record of the original arrangement.

"Now, I think, we might start," said Mr Blasterman.

"Not *really*?" Rodney muttered sarcastically. His father stepped forward and began to chip away the mortar.

It was slow dusty work, rather dull. Mr Walsh dared not work at his normal speed – he had the librarian peering anxiously over his shoulder. Debby's father stood, a patient giant, waiting for each lump of stone to be loosened so that he could heave it across the cellar and stack it with its number visible.

Sam Drake hovered, then, seeing that no harm would come to his precious wine, slipped away to catch up on some of his other jobs.

For the boys and girls there was nothing to do, nothing to see but the crouched figures of their elders through the dust haze. There were just too many of them in this confined space. Sheila was thankful when her father came back.

"Time for a break, Mr Blasterman?"

"I've brought coffee and stuff," she said quickly, "it's just upstairs."

"With a drop o' something else for the older ones," said her father, "with Mr Peblow's compliments."

The men seemed quite ready for the break. They had taken out five good-sized blocks, leaving a gap in the wall at shoulder height. Mr Harker had poked the broom through at the full length of his arm and met only emptiness. They had shone torches in but could see nothing. Until they had enlarged the hole and could climb through they would know no more.

They were glad to tramp upstairs to the daylight and fresh air. Sheila's mother had cut sandwiches and filled flasks with coffee. Her father had set out cans of beer.

She was glad to see him so bright again, doing the honours and talking proudly of "our" firm with its long history. Poor Dad, she thought, he's forgotten that next week it may not *be* "our" firm. He'll be working out his notice, but it won't really be Peblow's any more. It'll be on the way to demolition – not the demolition of a little wall but the real thing with bulldozers and everything. Another bit of the old city gone for ever. And all to make profits for some development company.

The men gossiped and laughed over their beer. Only Mr Blasterman fidgeted and looked at his watch. He wanted to get on, but those who were doing the hard manual labour had earned their breather. He didn't like to say anything. Nor did the young people.

It was the polite Kanshi who suddenly broke in. "Where's Debby?" he asked.

Chapter Eleven

During the coffee break Debby had been even more restless than her friends.

Twenty minutes earlier, when her father carried the fifth of the loosened stones across the cellar, she had looked at the hole and thought, I bet *I* could get through there now, even if no one else could.

As the men went on with their endless chit-chat over the beer her impatience became more than she could stand.

She glanced at Sheila and the boys. Should she whisper her idea? Better not. Sheila would want to ask permission. Then Mr Blasterman would start his boring talk about the importance of adult supervision.

So she quietly slid out from among them. No one made a murmur. Light-footed as a leopard she ran down the steps.

Under the arch the gap in the masonry winked at her invitingly, a dark eye hinting at mystery.

She measured it mentally. To other people it was still a narrow slit, but she was sure that her rubbery little body could wriggle through. There was a tiresome old school joke, that Debby Harker was "bottomless".

She laid her hands on the gritty edge. With a gymnast's ease she swung herself up. As she had guessed, the gap was wide enough for her shoulders. Thrusting through, she could flash her torch in all directions, see all that there was to see.

That wasn't much. Bare rock faced her, ten feet away. The inner cave looked disappointingly empty – no chests of treasure, no grinning skeletons in fetters sprawled about the floor. But at least she could *see* the floor – safe, solid and sandy. With a bit of twisting she could squirm through and drop down inside.

It might be worth doing. The rock wall opposite curved away to the left into a darkness that her torch beam could not penetrate. There might be something more interesting round that bend. If so, she'd be the first to find it.

So – why wait till the men had enlarged the hole enough to let their hulking bodies through? She'd better not dally. Any moment now they'd come tramping down again.

Even for her it proved a tight squeeze. It called for all her talents as a contortionist. But determination was rewarded. After a minute of breathless muscular manipulation she was through the breach, landing noiselessly on the floor within.

She straightened up, dusting her hands, and pulled out her torch again. Coo! It *was* a bit spooky, now that she was inside.

She was not scared, not really, though her heart seemed to beat faster. Just exertion, of course. Nothing to be frightened of. Her pa and the others were not far away. Now she had got through before they could stop her it was nice to know that soon they'd be back within call.

Should she startle them by speaking suddenly from this inner cave? Put on a spooky voice? Dracula, say?

71

Better not, perhaps. Her pa might say it wasn't funny at all. Anyhow, it was more urgent to take a look round before any one arrived.

The tiny flashlight threw only a weak white beam across the spaciousness she now sensed in front of her. She advanced cautiously to the left. No human foot had trodden this soft dry sand for centuries.

Suddenly the torch picked up a lumpish shape against the rock face. She stole towards it, heart in mouth. There was a cloth, which shredded away like a giant cobweb at the touch of her fingers. Underneath was a sort of box. A wild hope soared. What if Rodney had been right after all about treasure?

It was just a roughly made ordinary old box. Not even locked. She flashed her torch inside. It was stuffed with old papers. No writing, except for a brief scribble here and there in an old-time unreadable script. Sketches, more like. An artist's sketches?

She left them untouched. She advanced further, swinging the pale torch beam to left and right, probing for the furthest limits of the cave. The air was cold, dry and dusty as her movements stirred it – the first movements it had known since the day when Matthew Venner cemented the last block of stone into place.

Why had he taken all that trouble? The sense of disappointment grew upon her. Rod's dream of a treasure cave was a dead loss. Silly. Nothing here but a box of old sketchy drawings. Why build that massive wall?

Suddenly gold flashed at her in the white circle of her torch.

It twinkled at her at eye level, above the thrall, the

72

ancient stone shelf that had once carried the barrels of the medieval inn. Little points and patches of bright gold glinted like stars in a winter sky.

She stood rooted to the spot, trying to make sense of what she saw. Then, as she swung the arc of the torch further to the left, she saw something else.

She screamed. A dreadful face, a man's face, stared at her, spectral white. She spun round in panic and ran. She must reach the hole in the wall, somehow escape from this place of horror.

As she fled, the cave floor seemed to open beneath her. She pitched forward, the torch flying from her hand. She screamed again as she went down. Then the cave was silent, as it had been for the past four hundred years and more.

Chapter Twelve

Debby's absence did not at first cause any alarm.

"She's likely gone to the toilet," said Mr Harker.

Sheila was doubtful. "She'd have asked me where it was." She went along the passage. The lavatory was unoccupied. Nor was Debby in the yard. The heavy gates were unlocked, but they were closed. It did not look as though Debby had gone out into the street.

She called down the cellar steps. "Debby? Are you there? We're not supposed — " There was no reply.

She ran back to the others, seized by a sudden anxiety. Her father looked up crossly. "Can't you find her?"

"No, Dad — "

"I bet she's down in my cellars," said Mr Drake with grim disapproval. He clattered down the steps and Sheila followed. There was no sign of the black girl. He marched over to the hole in the archway. Sheila said, "She *could* have got through."

"You reckon so?"

"Debby could. You'd be surprised. It would be just like her to try."

He poked his head into the gap and bellowed, "Debby? Are you in there?"

Only an echo came back. His voice, not hers.

The cellar behind them filled with the rest of the party. Debby's father shouted, "Deb, you young monkey! If you're playing one o' your tricks — "

Again an echo. Then silence.

"I'll just check again upstairs," said Mr Drake. Sheila hurried after him. She felt guilty, but her father brushed aside her apologies. "You can't be responsible for everything your friends get up to." She felt guilty all the same.

Debby wasn't in the shop or Mr Peblow's office or anywhere on the ground floor. Nor was she upstairs in any of the stockrooms.

"She never said a word to me," said Sheila. "Her dad will be wild with her. Where can she be – unless — "

She did not like to finish the sentence. Suppose Debby *had* gone through that hole in the wall – and could not answer their shouts because something had happened to her?

They went down again and reported their failure to the others. What next? Carry on and enlarge the hole in case the girl *had* squeezed through? The question was settled for them. A thin little cry floated from far away.

"Help! He-elp! Oh, somebody, *please!*"

"That's her!" cried Mr Harker thickly. He thrust his great head into the aperture. "Where are you, honey? Are you hurt?"

"No, Pa, I — I'm OK. I banged my head. I think I knocked myself out."

How distant she sounded! Sheila wondered if it was another strange sound effect of this subterranean world.

"Give me that big torch," said Mr Harker. Rodney passed it and he projected its powerful beam into the cave beyond. "Can you walk back to the hole?" he called.

"Can you see this light I'm shining?"

"Only a dim sort o' flicker on the roof." Debby's answer sounded shaky. "I think I've fallen into some sort o' pit. And I can't get out."

"Then stay where you are, honey." Sheila thought to herself that her friend did not seem to have much choice. "Sure you haven't hurt yourself?" Mr Harker's deep voice was full of concern. "Not broken anything?"

"No, Pa, I'm OK, really I am."

"We'll have you out in a jiff, then."

No more talk of slow and scientific excavation. Rodney's father and Debby's attacked the masonry as though it were an enemy stronghold.

Through all the frantic thudding and clonking they could hear Debby singing – not her usual pop favourites but hymns, the rousing rhythmic type of hymn that her church preferred to the doleful dismal kind. It was no doubt Debby's way of keeping up her spirits until she was rescued.

The breach was widening fast. Sheila felt sure that she herself could squeeze through, to reach Debby and comfort her, but her father sternly forbade her. He wanted no more accidents.

Mr Walsh said quietly, "It's for you to say, Sam, but it'll take time before any of *us* can get through. My Rodney would go – he's sensible, he'll test every step of the way, won't you, Rod?"

"Sure thing, Dad!"

"Well, he's your boy," said Mr Drake. "I see your point. That poor girl must be scared out of her wits in there."

Rodney was eager to try. He pressed himself into the

jagged cleft. Sheila thrust a tube of sweets into his hand. "Take her these," she whispered.

He felt the stone hard and unyielding against his ribs. He strained desperately, swivelling a fraction of an inch to reduce his width. Then he was through.

"I'm coming, Deb!" he gasped. "Where are you?"

"Over here," she answered joyfully, "but do watch out."

She sounded much nearer now, but her voice came up from some depth in the darkness. He advanced gingerly, his torch trained on the sandy floor in front of his feet.

Debby talked on, anxious lest he make some fatal mistake. "It's like a great bowl in the rock," she said. "I don't know how deep – I lost my torch when I fell. But the sides are too smooth to climb out. There's nothing to get hold of."

"Relax," he said soothingly. "Your dad will be here in a minute, soon as he and my dad can widen the hole a bit. They'll fetch a ladder if we need it."

Debby sounded almost under his feet. The questing torch beam reached the edge of the pit – a smooth, curving rim, the tawny sandstone cut almost sheer below it, like the sides of a bowl.

He saw her dark head no vast distance down. Her teeth flashed in a grin of relief as she stared up at him, blinking in the light. She was standing in the centre of the pit. It was no great depth, but he could see why she had been unable to clamber out.

"Mercy you didn't break something," he said.

"It's quite soft on the bottom. Your feet sink in. Can't even do one of my running jumps."

Muffled shouts from the wine cellar reminded him that her father must be desperate for news. "Just a tick," he said, "I must report back."

"Don't leave me, Rod!" Her voice had altered suddenly, it had taken on an accent of terror.

"I'm not leaving you. But I must tell them you're OK."

"Be quick then. I want to get out o' here. I'm scared."

"Sheila sent you some sweets." He held them up in the light, then threw them. She caught them deftly.

"Thanks a lot," she said shakily.

He had to leave her in the dark, he dared not throw her the torch. He had to watch out for any further hazards on the way back. She began to sing another hymn. He knew now why she wasn't singing pop songs. She was defending herself against evil. He could not guess quite what.

He reached the hole in the wall, saw the men's tense faces staring through. "She seems OK," he said, "but I can't pull her out. I think it's one of those medieval malt kilns," he added for Mr Blasterman's benefit, "like the one they found in Castle Gate." The librarian would understand exactly what they were dealing with.

"And she ain't broken any bones?" demanded Mr Harker.

"No, she says it's soft at the bottom. Her feet sink in."

"When they stopped using the pits for malt," said Mr Blasterman, "they often turned them into rubbish dumps. We might find something interesting. Old pottery and so on." With Debby's safety assured his historical interests became uppermost again.

"I'd best get back. I promised. She's real scared."

"Say we're coming, quick as we can," said Mr Walsh.

The chipping and hammering were resumed. Rodney hurried back.

"Am I glad to see you!" she cried as the torch caught her in its circle of white light. "Am I glad to see anything!"

He'd always thought of her as absolutely fearless. It wasn't surprising that the fall had shattered her confidence, but the Debby he knew would have bounced up again like a ball. Her continuing nervousness puzzled him.

He must go on talking, keep her steady somehow till their fathers arrived. "How did it happen?" he asked.

She stared up at him with furrowed brow. "I'm trying to remember. It's – difficult. I cracked my head, falling. I think I was right out for a minute or two."

"But before that?" he prompted her.

She hesitated. "I thought I saw gold — "

"*Gold!*"

"There were all these angels — "

"Angels?" he echoed again. "How d'ye mean, angels?"

"But there was this horrible face glaring at me! Pale as death – only there was this red blood round his neck. I tried to run – but the floor just opened — "

At this point the cave filled with a babble of excited voices as the whole party came pouring through the gap. Debby looked up at a ring of torches and friendly faces.

"She's concussed or something," Rodney muttered to her father. "Been seeing angels, she says – and a horrible face."

"We'll get her out o' this," said Mr Harker.

Sheila's father had brought a step-ladder, but the

big black man did not wait for it. He dropped lightly into the pit and gathered Debby in his arms. Only then did she start to cry.

"Come on, honey. Here's a ladder. Mr Drake will give you a hand when you get to the top."

It was odd to see Debby, the champion gymnast, being fussed over like some old lady.

Up to now all lights had been focused on the pit. Only when Debby was hauled to safety did her rescuers pay any heed to their surroundings.

Kanshi was the first to let his torch beam flit along the wall of the cave. He let out an excited cry.

So did Debby. But hers was more than excited. It was tinged with terror.

"It's that face again! That dreadful face!"

Spotlit by half a dozen converging torches it was certainly a startling sight. The life-sized carving of a bearded face, the pallid alabaster tinted with colours, and beneath it a wavy blood-red line.

Mr Blasterman was the first to find words. "John the Baptist," he announced calmly. "The speciality of the alabastermen. They carved them by the score, sent them all over the place. Almost mass produced."

"Mass produced?" said Kanshi in a disappointed tone.

"Not this one," the librarian assured him with enthusiasm. He stepped forward to examine the sculptured tablet propped against the wall. "It's much bigger than usual. Remarkably powerful! The work of a real artist, not a journeyman. It proves what I've always suspected – Barwell was in a class by himself." He turned to Debby. "I don't wonder it gave you a turn.

After all, he *had* had his head cut off. It's standing in a pool of blood."

"Ugh!" said Sheila.

Mr Blasterman seemed specially thrilled by that gruesome line of scarlet. "See how the dry atmosphere has kept the original brightness of the paint? We know they used to colour their carvings, but you usually find only faint traces. This is a wonderful discovery!"

There was something even more wonderful to come. Rodney was playing his torch beam further round the side of the cave. Suddenly the gold flashed back at him.

"*Gosh!*" he yelled.

"The little angels!" cried Debby. "So I *did* see them – it wasn't just fancy."

Their crowns and wings, their harps and trumpets, glittered in the lights trained on them.

Tilted against the rock face, standing on the barrel thrall that ran along in front of it, were ranged a series of oblong slabs, each a picture of angelic figures cut deep into the alabaster. Besides the rich gilding the tablets were vivid with colour, red and blue, black and green and white. Each was different, but all had the same background of green, spangled with formal little daisies, painted with five white blobs and a red one in the middle.

Mr Blasterman was almost beside himself. "*Ten* panels!" he cried. "Unbelievable! There were usually only five or seven." They were, he explained, the separate parts of some great altarpiece designed to be fixed to the wall of a church or cathedral. The panels made for ease of transport to distant places. He had heard of only one ten-panel altarpiece, in France, but that one had lost its original colouring long ago.

"This one'll be worth something?" suggested Mr Drake.

"It'll be worth a packet," said Mr Walsh.

This aspect of the matter had not apparently occurred to Mr Blasterman. "Oh, yes," he agreed. "Alabaster carvings get auctioned at Sotheby's – but there's been nothing the size of this. It's the artistic quality that interests me, though – it's a masterpiece — "

"I reckon we ought to ring Mr Peblow," said Mr Drake.

"Certainly we must. At once."

Kanshi was measuring the slabs and scribbling notes. "Twenty-three angels," he announced.

"Aren't you going to count the daisies?" said Rodney. But Kanshi was too absorbed to be teased.

"This'll certainly fetch something," said Rodney's father, still pondering the cash value of the discovery. "Sort of thing people get up an appeal for – save it for the nation, and all that."

Mr Blasterman was moving off to make the telephone call. "All this will be Mr Peblow's property," he said. "I don't think it will count as treasure trove."

At that moment a stern voice boomed from the outer cellar.

"This is the police. Come out, one at a time – and don't try any funny business!"

Chapter Thirteen

It was hard to say who was more surprised – the excavators to find the outer cellar crowded with blue uniforms, or the policemen to see them file out through the demolished wall, four schoolchildren, three accompanied by their fathers, and the respected (if somewhat dusty) figure of Mr Blasterman from the public library.

Tension quickly relaxed as Mr Drake assured the sergeant that he was employed by Peblow's and had permission for what they were doing.

"I was about to telephone Mr Peblow," said the librarian.

"You do that, sir. I'll come with you if I may and have a word myself."

"As you please, Sergeant."

"I'll have to report the incident, you see. We got a 999 call. Suspicious noises underground. We thought we'd got a break-in to deal with – someone digging through to the jeweller's next door, to get into the strong room. Bank Holidays are a great time for break-ins at business premises."

Sheila's father took them both up to the office. The others waited awkwardly in the wine cellar, the policemen friendly but wary, and nobody else sure that it was all right to go. Not that anyone wanted to. It was all far too exciting.

After a few minutes the sergeant came down again with Sam Drake and Mr Blasterman. His manner had changed. The last sign of suspicion had gone and he seemed keenly interested.

"Perhaps I could have a look at this thing, sir — "

"Altarpiece," said the librarian a trifle sharply.

"Of course, sir. While we're waiting for Mr Peblow — "

"By all means. You won't have seen anything like it. I doubt if you ever will again." Mr Blasterman's eyes gleamed.

He led the way. The policemen followed. The fathers strung behind, the young people at their heels. Debby had now quite got over her nervousness. The terrifying face was only sculpture.

"How did you get on to this, sir?" asked the sergeant admiringly, when they had all exclaimed over the brilliance and beauty of the carved panels.

"Oh, one thing led to another. Like police enquiries!"

"I wish our enquiries led us to things like this."

Mr Blasterman was very fair in giving the schoolfriends the credit for starting the investigation. "I only came into it by chance, when we stumbled on a link with my own pet subject – the history of the local alabaster trade." He quoted the mysterious letter which the carver had written to the London merchant.

"*I thank you most heartily for the warning, and have followed your counsel ... Unless Joshua blow his trumpet again, the secret will be safe. It is fit that a great angel should shelter smaller angels under his wing.*"

The policemen murmured approvingly when Rodney described how they had puzzled over what the clues could mean, Joshua's trumpet and the "angels" which might prove to be gold coins. "Seems you've hit on

84

something just as good," said one man.

It was dawning on everybody that they had. Mr Blasterman said that the alabaster angels might be of unique value.

Nor were they the only find. As the constables prowled round, flashing their torches into every cranny with professional zeal, other items were revealed. Besides the horrific head of John the Baptist there were several exquisite statuettes, less than a metre high, depicting the Madonna and other biblical characters. These too had kept the pristine brilliance of their paint and gilding.

Mr Blasterman's excitement was redoubled. "The lost images from Venner's porch! So they *weren't* destroyed. These should go back to the parish church. I'm sure Mr Peblow will agree."

Finally there was the box of old papers Debby had seen. The librarian became almost delirious as he riffled through them and held them up in the light.

"These look like artist's sketches ... Goodness! The design for the whole altarpiece, section by section!"

"I wonder", said the sergeant, "that someone hid all this, building that wall and everything, but never came back for it — "

"I can tell you why," cried Mr Blasterman, waving the sheet of paper he had just picked up. This was covered with faded handwriting. "Listen to this! It's the actual letter the merchant had sent to Barwell – the letter he was answering." Slowly and jerkily, frowning over the crabbed script with its flourishes and archaic spelling, he read it aloud.

"As to the altarpiece commissioned for the great church of

St Michael and All Angels, I would counsel you that, since it cannot in this winter season be shipped across the seas to Spain, you do not yet send it to me but bestow it in some secret place, for it now stands in a greater peril even than shipwreck. The young King's advisers wax ever more furious against the old religion and what they term its superstitious images. There was an Act yesterday passed in Parliament, demanding that all such images be defaced and destroyed by the last day of June. It would be a great pity if this work of yours — "

"I needn't read any more," said the librarian.

"We've got the point," said Rodney's father.

"So had Barwell – as we know from his reply. He shifted his masterpiece down into this cellar under the Golden Angel inn, and his mason friend, Venner, walled up the entrance. Lucky they did it just in time. 1550! Think of what happened that year. The churches were stripped of all their statues. They were ruthlessly smashed. The alabaster ones were used to make plaster of Paris. The craft in this town was ruined for ever."

Of course, Mr Blasterman went on, other people thought of hiding their statuettes and panels. Even today they were still found occasionally under church floors and in similar places. That was why English alabaster could still be seen in museums.

"But nothing like this," he insisted. "The size of the work! The quality of the carving! And of course the *condition*, the colouring especially, thanks to the dry air!"

"So this Barwell never dared bring it out again?" asked the sergeant.

"He was very unlucky. The young King only lived

86

another three years, and his half-sister Mary became Queen — "

"Bloody Mary!" said Rodney with gusto, in case the policemen were weak on history.

"She brought back the old religion as fast as she could – but Barwell had died a few months earlier, and Venner a little before that. So the secret died with them."

"Until *we* — " began Rodney triumphantly.

Just then Mr Peblow and his daughter entered the cave.

Chapter Fourteen

Again there were gasps of amazement. Again Mr Blasterman had to repeat his potted history of Tudor religious conflicts and their catastrophic results for the alabaster men.

"To think," said Mr Peblow, "we've been working all these years with *this* just under our feet!"

"And you say it's really valuable?" said Miss Jenny.

"It is indeed," said the librarian.

"This'll be a newspaper story," said the sergeant. "It'll be on TV. You'll have to think about security, Mr Peblow, so long as these sculptures remain on the premises."

"Who's going to pinch all this lot?" Rodney muttered to his friends. "It must weigh tons."

The sharp-eared sergeant overheard him. "You'd be surprised, lad, what some of those villains can shift if there's big money to tempt them."

"It would be valueless to them," said Mr Blasterman. Every one stared. "They couldn't dispose of it. This is an art treasure. Once photographs are published it will be recognised anywhere. Which reminds me — " he turned to Kanshi " — it would be wise to get some pictures immediately."

Kanshi scuttled away with his camera. The sergeant had his notebook out and was asking routine questions.

"I'll have to make a report, explaining it was a false

alarm and giving the facts. There may have to be an inquest."

"An inquest?" echoed Miss Jenny. "There's no body."

"No, miss, but they'll need to decide if this is treasure trove and the property of the Crown — "

Gently but firmly Mr Blasterman interrupted. "I fancy they'll realise at once that this can't be. The law of treasure trove applies only to gold and silver articles. There's no silver here, no gold beyond the tiny fraction in the gilding. Carved stone hardly fits the definition of treasure trove. I think you will find that the whole lot will belong to Mr Peblow as the owner of the premises."

Miss Jenny's face lit up. "What a wonderful man you are, Mr Blasterman! You seem to know everything."

"Oh, no, but I'm a librarian. I know where to find things."

"You can say that again, sir," said the sergeant jovially. "You've done it today, anyhow." He scribbled. "It's not for me to say about the law of treasure trove, but no doubt you're right. I've only to report what's happened. I take it, Mr Peblow, you are the owner of these premises?"

"Oh, yes. For the moment at least." There was a slight hesitation in the wine merchant's voice.

"Thank God you haven't signed anything," murmured his daughter. No one asked what she meant. Sheila knew.

The cellar began to empty. The constables left. The sergeant followed Mr Peblow to his office. From the sounds of clinking glass and poppling liquid it appeared that he was stretching the regulations a little.

Miss Jenny did not forget the rest of them. She came

90

bustling out with a tray of glasses. "I think you all deserve champagne," she said gaily. "I hope you gentlemen will have no objection — "

"I won't, for one," said Rodney's father with a twinkle.

"I was going to say, no objection if, in the circumstances, your children join us?"

"Not so long as they leave some for us," said Debby's pa.

The corks popped like miniature explosions. The golden wine spumed into the slender glasses.

Miss Jenny smiled round at them all. She *was* good looking, thought Sheila. Funny that she'd never got married.

"I drink to all of you," she said. "You don't know what this may mean to us. But when it's all sorted out, if what Mr Blasterman says is right, my father will want to offer you a more tangible token of his gratitude."

The champagne was tangible enough, Sheila decided, as she took a swig and began to splutter.

The sergeant emerged from the office looking very benevolent and wished them a genial farewell. Mr Peblow joined the crowd. Mr Blasterman was whispering something to Miss Jenny. Rodney caught the words, "That's only my estimate, of course, based on the amounts paid at auctions in bygone years. Prices have shot up since then. And what we've found this morning is absolutely exceptional. Out of this world."

At that moment there was an unwelcome interruption. Simon Peblow came storming in from the street.

"What on earth is going on, Father? I called in to see you at home – I was sent down here – I see a police car driving away – and now some sort of drinking orgy — "

"I think you had better come into the office," said Mr Peblow with dignity.

"Excuse us a moment," said Miss Jenny to the others, hurrying after them and closing the door. But the voices within were soon so loud that it was impossible not to catch fragments of the argument.

"I have signed nothing – and I *shall* sign nothing," Mr Peblow kept repeating. "There will be no need, now."

"But on Saturday you as good as promised!" Simon shouted.

"You bullied him!" Miss Jenny's voice came through above the deep-toned wrangling of the men. "You – with your passion to get your hands on ready money!"

"He shall have his ready money." Mr Peblow was taking command of his contentious family at last. Son and daughter fell silent. Though he lowered his own voice his words were clearly audible to the others in the shop. They tried to make conversation among themselves, but it was hard to ignore the drama that was taking place.

"This discovery alters the whole situation," said the wine merchant. "I shall be able to give Simon this lump sum he is so eager for – *now*. He won't need to wait impatiently for me to die. I shall have done my duty by you, my boy, but not another penny will you ever get. I shan't need to sell out. Peblow's will continue. But after my time it will pass exclusively to your sister. That will be your share, Jenny my dear, and well you will deserve it."

Sheila looked across the shop and caught her father's eye. The relief in his face showed that he too had heard and understood. His own job was safe.

The office door was wrenched open. Simon Peblow stood there, snarling some ill-humoured farewell. Mr Peblow faced him calmly, holding a long, typewritten document. Very deliberately he tore it across, and across, and again across, before he tossed the pieces into his wastepaper basket.

Simon strode out, ignoring the clustered audience. They heard his car go roaring away down Gillyflower Hill.

Miss Jenny came out, flushed but smiling, followed by Mr Peblow. "Now, Father, you have a chance to say thank you to all these kind and helpful people."

The wine merchant rose to the occasion. Having shaken hands warmly with the men, he made for the young people. He complimented them on the perseverance and intelligence they had shown in their investigation.

"You've been good – *very* good," he said emphatically. "And who knows?" He surveyed their grinning faces with a twinkling eye. "Perhaps – like my wines – you will grow even better with age?"

Geoffrey Trease
Aunt Augusta's Elephant £2.99

Clearing out their great-aunt's flat in Bath, Nicola and Tim discover
an amazing enamel egg, wrapped in a yellowing scarf.

It's the most beautiful thing they have ever seen.

But they don't know then how much trouble the egg is going to
cause – nor how it would change their lives for ever . . .

'Aunt Augusta's Elephant is itself a delicately detailed little treasure'
THE GUARDIAN

Geoffrey Trease
The Popinjay Mystery £2.99

Charles II holds court in London and Sam Pepys holds the key to
Britain's sea-defences at the Navy office. Both men are surrounded
by political corruption and intrigue.

When young Lieutenant Denzil Swift rides to help rescue Pepys and
his companions from Highwaymen, he finds himself at the centre of
a desperate plot which threatens the fragile stability of the realm.

This fast-paced adventure reaches a thrilling climax in a river chase
on the Thames at high tide, midnight.

Geoffrey Trease
Tomorrow is a Stranger £2.99

WAR LATEST!
GERMANS INVADE THE CHANNEL ISLANDS!
British citizens now living in Occupied Territory.

After the wartime invasion of the Channel Islands, the few children left on Guernsey find life hasn't changed very much – not to begin with.

Paul and Tessa still have to go to school despite the German soldiers on the streets and barbed wire surrounding the town.

But then their teacher disappears. Suddenly there is danger and the war is frighteningly close.

Humphrey Carpenter
Crazee Teevee £4.99

Have you ever thought how boring a lot of the programmes on TV
are?

How about setting up your own TV station using your neighbours to
help out?

That's exactly how Crazee Teevee comes about – all you need is a
granny with a kitchen, a few friends and an eccentric do-it-all boff
for some great TV and hilarious adventures.

Rumer Godden
Mr McFadden's Hallowe'en £2.99

Hallowe'en is a special time in Scotland. Boys and girls dress up as ghosts, witches, bats and black cats and go visiting round the houses.

'I will be a good witch,' said Selina.

'There's no such thing,' said her sister Muffet.

But there was, and she brought good luck with her – to the village, to poor young Tim, but especially to Mr McFadden, the cross, friendless old farmer.

This was certainly one Hallowe'en *he* would never forget.

Dick Cate
Alexander and the Star Part £2.99

'Mooo-er'

'Mooo-urgh'

'Fabulosogargle'·

'Shut up'

'Ba-aaah'

'Wuff-wuff!'

'Shut . . . finally . . . UP!!'

Right from the very start it's *obvious* that the only miracle in
Alexander's school nativity play will be if it ever actually happens.

With the terrible Archie Poulson (playing one of the oxen wrapped
in a hearth rug) attacking one of the sheep . . . angels falling off their
stepladders . . . and Miss Tinson turning purple with rage . . .

. . . Alexander will have to act like mad to save the day!

Dick Cate
Alexander and the Tooth of Zaza £2.99

'Keep calm everyone, please! Shut up and stop shouting! Now . . .
everybody move into the dining room for trifle! Move!'

If there's anything worse than a birthday party you don't want to go
to, it's being ordered around when you get there!

All Alexander could do was wait for the moment when he could
swipe the largest cherry trifle from right under Eric Polecat's nose.
Then things started to happen. In came the Nagasaki Knee-Jerk . . .

. . . and out came Zaza's tooth!

Sarita Kendall
Ransom For A River Dolphin £2.99

For the people who live along the River Amazon, dolphins are
magical animals . . .

When Carmenza finds a badly injured dolphin, she remembers the
harpoon her step-father lost on his last fishing trip. She knows he
doesn't understand the dangers of using a dolphin's tooth as a lucky
charm . . .

Hidden among the trees at the edge of the lake, the beautiful pink
dolphin is nursed back to health by Carmenza and her classmate
Ramiro.

But it is only Ramiro's father, a wise old Indian, who can divert the
anger of the wounded dolphin's spirit . . .

Eva Ibbotson
Which Witch? £2.99

Which of the most powerful witches will win the right to marry
Arriman, the awful Wizard of the North?

The competition begins, and each witch in turn pulls out of the
cauldron her especially wicked spell. But some go terribly, horribly
wrong . . .

All Pan Books are available at your local bookshop or newsagent, or can be ordered direct from the publisher. Indicate the number of copies required and fill in the form below.

Send to: Pan C. S. Dept
              Macmillan Distribution Ltd
              Houndmills Basingstoke RG21 2XS
or phone: 0256 29242, quoting title, author and Credit Card number.

Please enclose a remittance* to the value of the cover price plus £1.00 for the first book plus 50p per copy for each additional book ordered.

*Payment may be made in sterling by UK personal cheque, postal order, sterling draft or international money order, made payable to Pan Books Ltd.

Alternatively by Barclaycard/Access/Amex/Diners

Card No.

Expiry Date

_____
Signature

Applicable only in the UK and BFPO addresses.

While every effort is made to keep prices low, it is sometimes necessary to increase prices at short notice. Pan Books reserve the right to show on covers and charge new retail prices which may differ from those advertised in the text or elsewhere.

NAME AND ADDRESS IN BLOCK LETTERS PLEASE

....

Name _____

Address_____

_____

_____

_____
3/87